California Nurses

Welcome to Leanora Paz Memorial Hospital!

Roommates Serena Dias and Avery Smith
have done it! They are *officially* qualified nurses.
And they're ready to hit the wards of
Leanora Paz Memorial Hospital and save lives!
While it's never easy to start a new job,
Serena and Avery are about to face more obstacles
than most new nurses. Because Serena has a
nine-month secret that she *can't* keep from surgeon
Tobias Renfro. And Avery has a billion dollar secret
that he *must* keep from Dr. Robyn Callaghan!

Escape to San Diego with...

Serena and Toby's Story
The Nurse's One-Night Baby by Tina Beckett

And

Avery and Roby's Story
Nurse with a Billion Dollar Secret by Scarlet Wilson

Available now!

D1048273

Dear Reader,

Where would we be without nurses? They play such an important role in health care and often go unappreciated. Or at least underappreciated. So as we celebrate International Nurses Day, think about all those people who give tirelessly of themselves when we tend to be at our most vulnerable. I am grateful for them.

Serena Dias is just such a nurse. She has crossed the finish line in her goal to become a nurse and goes out to celebrate. In the process, she meets a handsome stranger and has a very sexy night with him. Only she winds up with a little more than she bargained for. Not only does the man turn out to be a trauma surgeon at her new hospital…but she also soon finds out she's pregnant with his child.

Toby Renfro has reasons for not wanting to become a dad. But now, faced with the fact that it's happening whether he likes it or not, he has some tough decisions to make.

Thank you for joining this special couple as they tackle a surprise pregnancy and navigate all its implications. Could it be that this tiny hope of life will draw them together in unexpected ways?

Love,

Tina Beckett

THE NURSE'S
ONE-NIGHT BABY

——

TINA BECKETT

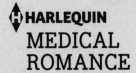

**MEDICAL
ROMANCE**

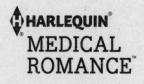

HARLEQUIN®
MEDICAL
ROMANCE™

ISBN-13: 978-1-335-73780-9

The Nurse's One-Night Baby

Copyright © 2023 by Tina Beckett

Harlequin Enterprises ULC
22 Adelaide St. West, 41st Floor
Toronto, Ontario M5H 4E3, Canada
www.Harlequin.com

Printed in U.S.A.

Three-times Golden Heart® Award finalist **Tina Beckett** learned to pack her suitcases almost before she learned to read. Born to a military family, she has lived in the United States, Puerto Rico, Portugal and Brazil. In addition to traveling, Tina loves to cuddle with her pug, Alex, spend time with her family and hit the trails on her horse. Learn more about Tina from her website or friend her on Facebook.

Books by Tina Beckett

Harlequin Medical Romance

The Island Clinic collection

How to Win the Surgeon's Heart

New York Bachelor's Club

Consequences of Their New York Night
The Trouble with the Tempting Doc

It Started with a Winter Kiss
Starting Over with the Single Dad
Their Reunion to Remember
One Night with the Sicilian Surgeon
From Wedding Guest to Bride?
A Family Made in Paradise
The Vet, the Pup and the Paramedic

Visit the Author Profile page
at Harlequin.com for more titles.

To the nurses in my family.
Thank you for all you do.

PROLOGUE

THE STROBING LIGHTS played tricks on Serena Dias's perceptions, imbuing everything around her with a feeling of disjointed sensuality. One that came in snatches that made her see stars. And every time the flash came, the people had shifted. Moved.

Danced.

Except one couple who appeared fixed in time, straining together as the world swirled around them.

Not quite what she'd expected from her celebratory night.

She'd long since lost sight of her cousin Amilda, but then again, Ami had already warned her not to expect to leave the bar together. Serena knew her well enough to take her at her word. Which left her alone in one of the wilder parts of her hometown of Cozumel.

And yet, it was perfect. Fit her mood to a tee.

Her time in nursing school had been much like this. Not the bar itself, but the atmosphere. Her memories of the grueling process of qualifying for—and then passing—that last licensing exam came in quick, stilted vignettes that depicted the passing of time. This trip to Mexico was a celebration of finally being legally allowed to use the coveted title of Registered Nurse.

She'd worked so, so hard. Surely she deserved to cut loose for one night?

Maybe she would have been better served by staying in San Diego and going to dinner with her hunky roommate, who'd also just finished qualifying. Then, at least, she could have pretended she had someone special in her life, even though she and Avery were just good friends.

Ah, to hell with it. She could celebrate on her own just as easily as she could with Ami or Avery or anyone else. She took one last pull of her frosty margarita and set it firmly on the bar. She was here to dance, and dance she would. With or without a partner.

Her first step had a slight wobble to it, only because Ami had talked her into wearing her sky-high pumps rather than Serena's own more sensible slingbacks. By her second step, though, she'd decided she was going to own the shoes and all they stood for.

Before she could, a man crossed her path and stopped dead in his tracks, giving her a once-over and a smile that told her in no uncertain terms what he was thinking. Her chin went up, and she shook her head, moving to step past him. Except one of her heels chose just that moment to hit the floor at a wonky angle before starting to slide sideways, gaining momentum.

Oh, God. She was going to fall. In slow, strobing motion.

But something caught her from behind. Not the leering stranger, who hadn't moved. And not some*thing*.

Some*one*.

A very solid, very steady someone. His arms were locked around her midsection, her back pressed against the entire length of him.

Oh. Wow.

She closed her eyes for a second, somehow not wanting to turn around and be disappointed by yet another leering stranger. But she owed him at least a thank-you.

Shifting, she somehow managed to tame her stilettos and get them back underneath her. She pivoted and blinked, finding a white button-down shirt. Craning her neck, her gaze followed the trail of buttons up past a tanned neck, a strong, square chin, until she met eyes that were startlingly blue.

Her mouth went dry, and she completely lost her train of thought.

"I… I… Oh…" She finally remembered what country she was in. *"Muchas gracias."*

He said something that she couldn't quite hear.

"Sorry?"

Damn. She'd done it again. She'd lived in the States so much of her life that now English came naturally, even though Spanish was her mother tongue.

"I said, 'you're welcome.'" He glanced pointedly over her shoulder before bending down. "Would you like to dance for a few minutes?"

He'd had to put his lips close to her ear

to be heard over the next round of music, and the low rumble of his voice sent a shiver over her.

She realized he was trying to help her avoid an uncomfortable situation with the guy who'd stepped into her path a few seconds ago. Through the blinks of light, she studied him for a second or two before something in his face satisfied her. He really was trying to help.

She nodded and let him lead her into the throng, leaving the other guy behind.

Thank God.

Except the second she went to lay her palms on this new stranger's shoulders, they slid behind his neck instead and linked there. If he noticed, he didn't say anything, those swoon-worthy eyes of his meeting hers before he leaned closer. "How steady are you on your feet?"

Was he asking if she was drunk? Ha! Not hardly.

Her brows went up. "Steady enough." As if to demonstrate her point, she took a step back, her right hand sliding down his arm until she found his fingers, an unspoken signal for him to twirl her. And twirl he did. Thankfully, her brain managed to trick her feet into doing exactly what she wanted them to do. When the rotation was complete and she'd settled back against his chest, she looked up at him in triumph, almost shouting to be heard over the rocker on the DJ's playlist. "See? Very steady."

Just as steady as the man's hands, his gaze…his body.

"So I see." One corner of his mouth lifted, and the sheer deliciousness of the act made her insides shimmy.

They stood there for a moment or two without moving, as the lights, the music, the people continued to swirl without noticing them.

But she noticed.

And suddenly, she knew exactly the kind of celebration she wanted. The celebration she needed. She bit her lip, trying to decide just how shocked he would be if she kissed him.

Not very, she decided. He was hot. Evidently unattached…and here.

She tried to go up on tiptoe, but the shoes already had her at maximum elevation.

But somehow, he seemed to know what

she wanted. Because as the lights flashed around her, his palm came up to cup her chin. He seemed to ask a question that she was only too eager to answer.

"Yes."

And then his mouth was on hers, one arm sweeping around her back to bind her to his hips. And that was all it took to seal her decision:

This man.

This venue.

This night.

CHAPTER ONE

TOBIAS RENFRO HAD made the right decision. For himself. For everyone.

Four weeks after his self-imposed honeymoon, he'd come back to the States with a renewed sense of commitment that the only thing he needed to be married to was his work. At least right now. Maybe even forever. All he lacked was a ring on his finger to seal the deal.

The fact that doubts about getting hitched had been boiling in his midsection for the past six months followed by the discovery that his fiancée Tanya had been embroiled in an affair with his best man had hammered home that he really needed to listen to his instincts.

And right now, his instincts were telling him to steer clear of women. All women, really. But especially those he worked with, like Tanya. Once had been more than enough for a lifetime.

Thank God Tanya and Cliff had decided to relocate to San Francisco so he wouldn't have to see them every day.

All in all, it was a good day. While in Mexico, he'd said his goodbyes to past mistakes in the best way possible. And vowed he wouldn't repeat them again. Ever.

Heading onto the floor to do his morning rounds, he glanced at the nurses' station and caught sight of a quick swirl of dark hair as someone turned and rushed down the hallway at the frantic pace of someone who'd been alerted to a Code Blue. Only there'd been no announcement of one. And there was something about the way she moved that set off alarm bells of a different type in his head. His steps ground to a halt as he glanced over at Jacelyn Webber, who was entering something into a computer at the desk. He headed over to her.

"Did we get a new nurse?"

"We did. I told you about that, remember?" She looked up and glanced behind her. "Well… We did have one. Hopefully the sight of you hasn't sent her running for the hills." The charge nurse smiled to take the sting out of the words. "You can look pretty intimidating when you want to."

He could? He paused for a second and shook his head. "I don't think I've run anyone off yet."

Except maybe Tanya. He gritted his teeth. No, he hadn't run her off. She'd taken off. With Cliff.

Jacelyn's smile widened, and Toby saw why she was so popular with her grandchildren. Warm and compassionate, her ready smile was contagious, and she was also a favorite with patients on the floor. "I'm kidding." She glanced again down the hallway. "Someone must have paged her. Anyway, her name is Serena Dias, and I think she's going to make a great addition to our department. She's fresh out of nursing school and very enthusiastic."

Serena? Something crunched its way through the confines of his skull, and he struggled to drag his attention back to Jacelyn still talking about the new nurse, who was evidently brimming with new ideas.

She was responsible for hiring in their department, and she hadn't steered them wrong yet. But what if, without realizing, she'd just dragged a memory back from Cozumel? A very hot memory.

What were the odds that…?

Astronomical. Odds were good that the name and the dark-haired woman he'd glimpsed had simply struck at the memory center of his brain and made him panic for a fleeting moment.

No, she wasn't *his* mystery woman. She was miles and miles away. In Mexico.

He forced himself to relax. "Good to hear."

"Yes. She actually just got back from visiting some of her family in Cozumel. That place is on my bucket list. Serena was actually born there, lucky girl."

Every muscle that had relaxed went back on high alert. "Cozumel? Are you sure?"

"Yep. As in Mexico."

The crunching sensation grew stronger until he couldn't hear anything else. His facial muscles somehow mustered a smile. "I do know where Cozumel is." He hadn't actually told anyone where he was going a month ago, preferring that no one relate it back to his honeymoon destination. It had been hard enough to get people to drop the words of sympathy over the sudden canceling of his wedding. Their knowing that he'd taken a solo trip to his honeymoon destination was bound to bring more pity he didn't want. Hell, Toby would have felt sorry for himself. Had, in fact. Until…her.

A movement caught his eye, and he saw the woman—dressed in scrubs—trudging back down the hallway, looking like she'd rather be anywhere but here. His stomach wound tight with dread. But no amount of damning the impulses that had put them together in his hotel bed would change anything. Because despite the odds, despite his pep talk that there was no way it could be her… There evidently *was* a way. Because he remembered this woman.

In stunning detail.

From the tiny butterfly tattoo on the outside of her left breast to the way she'd jerked on her clothes not long after their time together, saying she needed to go, that her family would worry if she didn't come home tonight.

All signs that he took to mean that she actually lived in Cozumel, despite the flawless

English that she'd slipped into a lot more easily than he'd expected.

She hesitated before lifting her chin and finishing her commute over to the desk. She stood next to Jacelyn, who glanced at her.

"Oh, good. I was wondering where you'd gone. Serena, I'd like you to meet one of our trauma surgeons. You'll be working pretty closely with him and his patients, since I know you spent a lot of time training in surgical procedures." She gave a half shrug. "Anyway, this is Dr. Renfro. One of our best."

Despite his best effort, his lips curved—this time of their own volition. He could tell from her face that she, too, would rather be anywhere but here. "Serena and I have already met, actually."

Her eyes went wide, and he could have sworn she shook her head, although Jacelyn wouldn't have noticed.

"You have?" The head nurse looked from one to the other.

There was another tiny hesitation before she held out her hand. "Yes. We, er, met around the time I graduated. I just didn't know he worked here. Nice to see you again, Dr. Renfro."

There'd been no doubt that her quick flight from the nurses' station had been due to her recognizing him. But if she was worried about him trumpeting about what had happened between them, she needn't. The fewer people who knew about his trip to Mexico, the better. But trying to pretend they'd never met before? It was easier just to admit it and go on. "Nice to see you as well. Is this your first day at Paz Memorial?"

He pressed her fingers to acknowledge her greeting, the contact sending him straight back to when he'd led her out onto that dance floor a month ago. Hell. Why did she have to be here, of all places?

Leonora Paz Memorial Hospital was often shortened to Paz Memorial among staff members. It had been built over thirty years ago as a memorial to the late wife of a wealthy businessman, the man having spent more than a billion dollars on the initial construction of it after her passing. The Paz family still owned the hospital today, and one of the businessman's children was the current chief executive officer.

"Yes. It's my first day."

Letting go of her hand, he kept his smile impartial, as if touching her hadn't sent a shaft of some weird impulse through him that he'd promptly squashed.

She hadn't sent him any sultry glances or hints that she'd like to take up where they'd left off. He was grateful for that. No more hospital romances for him. The less anyone knew about their encounter the better. And from the way she'd fled the nurses' station when she'd seen him coming, he doubted there would be any danger of her starting any rumors.

Not that either of them had done anything wrong. But, hell, if he'd known who she was in that bar, things would have ended very differently.

Oh, he wouldn't have turned his back on her if the creep who'd stepped in front of her had caused trouble. But he definitely wouldn't have spent the night with her. No matter how beautiful she was. No matter how in sync her body had been with his out on that dance floor. The whole night had had a surreal aspect to it, as if it had been dredged up from a dream.

But her standing here was living proof that what had happened had been all too real.

He forced himself to speak up and end this meeting in a professional way that set the tone for any future encounters between them. "Well, I hope your time at Paz Memorial proves a good start for a long career. If you have any questions, I'm sure Jacelyn or any of the other staff members will be more than happy to answer them." He purposely left himself out of the mix.

Jacelyn gave them a smile. "Do you want to show Serena the surgical suite, Toby? We haven't gotten that far this morning. Unless you're in the middle of something…" Her head tilted as if seeing something in his face.

So much for trying to play it cool. He could just say he needed to start on his rounds, which he did. But if he acted too anxious to get away from Serena, it would make Jacelyn wonder if there'd been something more to their initial meeting than either of them had admitted.

If only she knew.

"I'd be happy to," he lied. He sent Serena a polite smile and motioned to the left. "It's just this way."

The second they turned the corner, she whispered to him, "Why did you tell her we'd met before?"

"We had. To try to pretend otherwise would only make things harder in the end." Although he was beginning to wonder. He could have pretended he was too drunk to remember anything from that night. But somewhere, somehow, one of them was bound to slip up. And if he'd been worried about rumors before, there'd be a slew of them if someone overheard the wrong thing.

"Harder for who?"

"For both of us." He stopped to face her and took in the expression on her face. "Look, I'm sorry if my admitting that made you uncomfortable."

She leaned against the wall behind her, tipping her head back to rest against the solid surface. The act made the long line of her neck visible. His eyes couldn't resist tracing it for a second, memories of pressing kisses to that soft skin making him swallow hard.

"It's more than that. I… I… I've wanted to be a nurse for as long as I can remember. I don't want anything jeopardizing that."

Her words brought him back to earth with a bump. "You think I would do that?"

"Not on purpose." Her head came away from the wall and she looked up at him. "I just would rather no one know about what happened in Cozumel."

"Believe me," he said fervently. "I'd rather no one know that I was in Mexico at all."

This time her eyes narrowed. "Why?"

There was no way he was going to admit the reason for his visit. But he also didn't want her to think he was embarrassed about being there. And something in her voice said she was wondering that exact thing.

He reached out and touched her hand. "I have my reasons. But I assure you they have nothing to do with the country or you."

She studied him for a second before nodding. "Okay. So we'll just tell people we met casually and leave it at that."

"Exactly."

She squeezed his hand and released him. "Then we'd better head on to the surgical suite before someone sees us and wonders if there's more to it than that."

She was right. Jacelyn coming down the

hallway, and finding them like this would probably make her wonder. "Okay, let's go."

They headed on their way, both of them silent. He gave an internal sigh. Yes, working with her was going to be uncomfortable for a while. At least during this initial period as they struggled to find a way to deal with each other.

But those dealings would be entirely professional. At least on his end. And he was pretty sure from her stiff posture as she walked beside him that she would be just as happy to leave things at that.

Maybe he had jinxed himself by saying today was a good day so far. Because the day had just turned upside down and proved that he was right. His dealings with women always seemed to come back and bite him in the rear.

Which was exactly why he was going to make sure his actions and behavior gave Serena no hint that he wanted to continue what they'd started in Mexico. Because to him, it hadn't been the start of anything. It had been a kiss goodbye to the past, and the signal of a new start in his quest to devote his life to his job.

At least for now. Maybe someday that would change, but Toby didn't see it happening any time soon. And definitely not with Serena or anyone else from work.

That was one vow he was not going back on. Not now. Not ever.

Toby had been nothing if not distant over this last week, ever since their unexpected meeting at the nurse's desk. Nothing like the man she'd met in that bar in Cozumel. But that was a good thing. A very good thing.

Better than his trying to sidle up to her with some kind of offer to continue what they'd started on the sly. He hadn't done that at all. But that touch in the hallway had sent her pulse skyrocketing—as had the intimacy of their conversation. Even though there'd been no hint of his wanting anything else from her than a professional relationship.

Although at that moment, if he'd leaned a little closer and just…

She shook the thought free. She didn't see him doing that. It was one of the things that had attracted her to him that night. The fact that she'd sensed that one-night stands were as foreign to him as they were to her. And that he was as anxious as she was to put it behind her. It was why Toby had been able to lead her onto the dance floor while the leering man had left her completely cold.

Fortunately, life on the surgical floor had proved too busy for her to sit there and mull over thoughts of that night. At least not much.

He'd asked her how steady on her feet she was that night. She was beginning to wonder, because she still felt unsteady any time she was around him. She'd better figure out a way to get over that, and fast.

But at least he didn't seem to have it in for her or try to subtly pressure her to quit.

Why would he do that, though? They really hadn't done anything wrong. Out of character? Maybe. At least for her. But he'd made it clear he wasn't married and wasn't in the market for a relationship, which had been perfect for her, since she wasn't either. Nursing school had consumed her life for the last several years. In fact, her last semiserious relationship had been during her first year of college. But Parker's hint that she was too devoted to her future career had quickly extinguished her feelings for him. Her father had held her mom back from what she'd wanted in life, and her mom's resentment had been more than apparent for years. Serena never understood why she'd put up with it. She knew her mom didn't believe in divorce, but in some circumstances, Serena had to disagree.

When her dad had suddenly passed away five years ago, her mother had finally had the chance to emerge from her cocoon and fly. And fly she did. She became a writer who was both funny and poignant, and although she wrote Spanish fiction, Serena could definitely pick out the parts that touched on reality. And while she was happy for her mom, she wished her father had been more supportive of her talents while he was alive.

Serena had secretly had a butterfly tattooed in a place it wouldn't be seen to remind herself of her mom and how she needed to follow her mom's lead and transform her dreams into reality, to allow them to carry her away. And now, she was doing just that.

So she was in no hurry to link up with any man. She had a lot she wanted to accomplish in her own right. She was definitely not going to let her emotions take over the thinking center of her brain. No. If anything, she was going to overanalyze everything.

Even if Toby had tried to push her out, she wouldn't have gone down without a fight. She would not lose her career over one impulsive night. But he'd given no sign that he wanted any such thing. Which was a huge relief.

Turning the corner, she ran into the very man she'd been thinking about. Well, not literally, but they were walking toward each other. The sight of his mauve polo shirt and black pants made her tummy shift. It was different from the dark-washed jeans and button-down shirt he'd worn to the club in Cozumel. It was strange that even though he was in office attire, he looked less formal here than he had that night. Maybe because of the way he'd stared down that creep at the bar.

"Hi." Her voice came out slightly breathy, and she cringed at the sound. The last thing she wanted was for him to think she had some kind of crush on him. She didn't. Even though the time they'd spent together had taken on a dream-like quality that threatened to become entombed in her brain.

"Hello. How are you?"

"Good, thanks. Yourself?"

So far so good. This was about as impersonal as you could get.

"I'm good." He frowned slightly "Are you headed to Mabel Tucker's room, by chance?"

"I am. It's time to check her vitals and see how she's coming along after surgery." She had yet to share a surgical suite with the man, but that wasn't to say that she hadn't been in the operating room at all. She'd assisted in several procedures and found that she loved the charged atmosphere in there. She assumed that Toby had his own team that he preferred to work with.

Or maybe he didn't want to work with her at all after their last conversation.

Which suited her just fine. Although it was inevitable that they would work together, eventually. So she was just going to have to suck it up and get on with it. What she really needed to do was stop noticing every little thing about the man. Like those glacial blue eyes. And that short hair that had felt so warm and luscious that night…incredibly silky sliding through her fingers.

Oh, God.

Was that what had happened with her mom? She'd fallen in love before she'd properly gotten to know the man who would become her husband? Serena cleared her throat and realized the sound had been audible.

Toby's head tilted slightly. "Mind if I join you?"

She tensed. "Sorry?"

"Mrs. Tucker?"

Of course, that's what he meant. She needed to watch her step. If she acted put out or hesitant, he was going to pick up on it and wonder why. Except he'd been headed in the opposite direction from Mrs. Tucker's room.

The victim of a drunk driver, she'd perforated her spleen and had required emergency surgery late into the night.

"Sure. Didn't you do her surgery last night, though? I'm surprised you're here."

The half shrug he gave her was painfully familiar. He'd given her that same gesture when she'd said she had to leave his hotel room because her family would be worried. He hadn't tried to convince her to stay longer or spend the whole night with him. Kind of an "it is what it is" gesture that said it didn't matter one way or the other to him.

How could something so simple cause both relief and irritation?

Maybe because it reminded her of her mom's reaction when a teenage Serena had come across a binder of her mom's dream occupations. There'd been about twenty of them. Nurse had been at the top of the list. Serena had been shocked. She'd always thought the decision to stay at home and raise her and her brother had been her mother's choice. It was the first time she realized her dad's controlling tendencies had extended beyond her and Sergio.

When she'd gone to her mom with the binder and asked what it meant, and if she still wanted to become any of the things on that list, her mom had just lifted one shoulder and taken the book from her, carrying it back to her bedroom. She'd never seen it again. But it did cause her to pay more attention to her dad's behavior. And the little things she'd noticed bothered her more than she'd ever admitted.

"She's been in quite a bit of pain. Mrs. Tucker, that is."

He gave her a quick glance, and she tensed yet again. Of course, he knew who she was

talking about. She needed to pull herself together. She'd felt slightly off today, ever since
she'd woken up, and she wasn't sure why.

The surgeon pivoted, and they began
walking toward the patient's room. Serena
found herself hyperaware of the man. She
dissected everything about him, from his
clean scent to the loose, fluid way in which
he moved. Honestly, it irritated her that he
looked so well rested and fresh with no trace
of having pulled an all-nighter. On days that
she worked late, it was obvious to everyone.
Her eyes became bagged down with circles
and she tended to yawn incessantly.

Not this man. It was like he was perfection itself. But he wasn't. Somewhere in
there were flaws. Idiosyncrasies like that
half shrug. She just needed to remind herself of that fact.

They reached Mrs. Tucker's room thirty
seconds later, and Toby waited for her to go
through the door first and let her take the
lead once they were both inside.

A man stood almost immediately. "Hi, I'm
Tom, Mabel's husband."

"Good to meet you," Serena said. "And
good to see you again, Mabel. How are you

feeling this morning?" They'd given her another dose of pain meds an hour ago, and Serena had been monitoring her heart rate every time she checked in at the nurse's desk. The floor was super busy today. They had two other patients from the same vehicular accident. Five others had been transferred to other hospitals.

Tom sat back down at her bedside, holding her hand.

"My stomach still hurts pretty badly. And my head." Her voice was thready and weak, and unlike for Serena, whose dark circles were caused by lack of sleep, the darkness under this young woman's eyes was caused by the trauma of the accident. She'd shared with Serena that she'd turned her head, catching sight of movement coming at her from the side just in time to be hit by another car. It had slammed her head into the driver's-side window, breaking her nose and causing a concussion. And the force of the collision had caused several internal injuries, her damaged spleen being the most critical.

It had all happened so fast that it had caused a pileup on one of the city's main thoroughfares.

"Well, I brought Dr. Renfro with me. He's going to check you over once I get your vitals."

Aware that he was watching her, Serena was glad that her hands were steadier than her nerves. She wasn't sure why she was even rattled. She'd had doctors in the room with her before—even during nursing school—and had done just fine.

Mabel's blood pressure was a little low and her heart rate was up, but that made sense, since she'd lost quite a bit of blood volume through internal bleeding.

She said all the readings aloud for Toby's benefit as she entered them into the tablet that connected into the hospital's mainframe.

Then she stood back so that he could move up and do his own evaluation. Normally she would have checked the patient's incisions and bandages, but since he would just need to repeat all of that, she let him do it while she observed.

He was meticulous as he checked Mabel's pupillary responses and examined the large swelling on her forehead from where she'd hit the window. Then he moved on to her abdomen. When she'd arrived, she'd been critical, and there'd been no time to set up the laparoscopy equipment; they'd had to get her spleen out as fast as they could since it was dumping blood into her abdominal cavity.

"Where exactly does it hurt? Where the incision is?"

"Yes. And inside my belly." She winced as if something twinged. "Is that normal?"

He nodded. "It can be. Let me take a look. It's going to be a little uncomfortable, but it won't last long.

Her husband leaned closer. "Squeeze my hand tight, sweetheart." He kissed her fingers and then wrapped his hand around them.

"Ready?"

The woman nodded, her knuckles turning white as she squeezed and squeezed.

Toby's hands were gentle as he carefully lifted her gown and peeled away the taped dressing, examining the area with those glacial blue eyes that had probably looked at thousands of incisions. The area was pink with a normal amount of puffiness. No weeping. And those stitches… They were perfection. Each suture was perfectly spaced, and the line was perfectly horizontal. Her scar would be a fine line that—barring complications—would be barely noticeable.

"Here comes the hard part. Try to relax your muscles."

Serena found herself following his instructions in a sympathetic move that made her smile.

Toby caught her, head cocking a bit in question. She quickly shook her head to indicate it was nothing.

Turning back to his patient, he pressed into the soft tissue of her belly, and Mabel groaned, her eyelids squinching tight.

"Belly is soft. No evidence of a leaking vessel."

One of the worries after internal trauma was that a bleeder would be missed or that, like dominoes falling, another system would begin to fail.

He stood straight. "All done, Mabel."

She opened her eyes and blew out a shaky breath. "Is it okay? I dreamed my stomach was filling up with blood. And when I woke up, it hurt so bad, I was afraid…"

And it actually had been when she'd arrived at the hospital. The trauma to her mind was every bit as real as the trauma to her body.

Toby pulled the wheeled stool over and sat down next to his patient. Something pulled at Serena's insides. It would have been faster for him to stand over Mabel's bed and give her the rundown, but Serena was impressed that he clearly liked to get on the same level as his patient. Not all doctors did that.

"I'm not seeing anything that would make me think that. If there was any hint of it, I'd send you over for a CT scan. But I do want you to keep track of your pain levels and let your nurses know they can call me at any time. Day or night."

Mabel's eyes filled with tears, and her fingers loosened their grip on her husband's hand. "Thank you so much."

"You're very welcome. I'll be back to see you again before I leave for the day, okay?"

"Okay." The woman seemed to sink deeper into the mattress as her muscles loosened.

"Can I stay with her?" Tom asked.

Toby nodded. "Of course. The chair by the window folds almost flat." He smiled. "It's pretty comfortable, actually. Don't ask me how I know."

"I can get you a blanket, if you want," Serena offered.

"Thank you so much. Mabel was on the way to the airport to pick me up when the accident happened. I'm just glad she's going to be okay."

Serena smiled. "We all are. Any other questions?"

They both shook their heads.

"Well, try to get some rest. Both of you. They'll be coming to get you up out of bed in a little while, so sleep while you can," Toby said.

They said their goodbyes, and he held the door for her to exit.

"Thanks, Toby." Too late, she realized she'd addressed him by his first name. In fact, she'd thought of him by his given name ever since their encounter that first day at the nurse's desk. After Cozumel, it seemed silly to think of him as Dr. Renfro.

But although most other staff members called each other by their first names, she'd done her damnedest to address him in more formal terms. Until now. And it was impossible to go back and undo that damage.

Only now that she'd broken that first rule, she was going to have to make sure she didn't go breaking any others. Or she'd find herself exactly where she'd been in Cozumel: in Toby's arms, doing things that drove them both wild. There could be no more of that. In Mexico, she hadn't known who Toby was, so she could give herself a pass for sleeping with him.

But now that she knew? No more excuses.

So she was going to make sure she kept any attraction she felt for the man strictly under wraps. No matter how hard that might prove to be.

CHAPTER TWO

TOBY GOT HOME and dropped into a chair, his cat curling up on his lap as he sucked down a deep breath. He was exhausted. Even more so than normal. He stroked the feline's short fur and tried to figure out what was going on.

His tiredness wasn't just because of the surgery, although he'd been up for almost twenty-four hours straight. That was nothing new for him.

So why this bone-weary fatigue that seemed to swallowed him into the very fabric of his easy chair?

It was because every time he'd seen Serena today on the floor, he seemed to tense up with memories that were best laid to rest. Except that was proving impossible. And to be in an actual exam room with her? Hell, he'd had to fight to keep his mind on his patient. And that wasn't like him. At all.

He'd always been able to compartmentalize his life. Just like his parents seemed to be experts in doing. Only their compartment for displays of affection toward their son had seemed so small as to be virtually nonexistent. So for Toby to have a hard time containing his wild sense of excitement when he'd been confronted with the fact that Serena had joined Paz Memorial was unexpected. And entirely unwelcome.

What was going to happen the first time they shared an operating room?

Nothing. Because he was going to get his act together and figure out how to work side by side with her. Without the excitement. Or clawing urge to repeat that night in Cozumel.

And that was part of the problem. It had been one night. Not even an entire night, at that.

He'd been able contain his feelings for his ex while at work, and he'd been involved with Tanya for almost three years before they'd finally gotten engaged. He'd known Serena for how long? A week?

Well…a week and part of a night. A night that dreams were made of.

But not his dreams. At least not the permanent kind. So why had she fallen so eagerly into his arms? Was that what she usually did? Pick guys up in bars for brief encounters?

No. He'd seen the flash of uneasiness in her eyes when confronted by that man who'd obviously had only one thing on his mind.

So why Toby? Why spend the night with him? Not that she had. She'd flown out of his room like a bat out of hell, nothing like that tiny butterfly tattoo on her breast that he'd traced with his lips.

And licked.

He pinched the bridge of his nose. Hell. It wasn't the only thing he'd tasted.

And that was part of the problem. Their coming together had been chaotic. So fast. And yet, every second of it was burned on his brain. Drawn with an indelible ink that he knew would mark his psyche for a long time to come.

But he wasn't sure how to separate that night from the days he was going to spend working with her.

There would be a lot of those days. They

stretched out as far as the eye could see. And knowing he was never going to be able to touch her again like he had that night…

Well, hell, it shouldn't be as hard as it was.

Somehow he was going to have to figure it out, and fast. But for now, he decided he was too tired to move. Too tired to shower. Too tired to watch television.

And hopefully too tired to picture any more scenes that had Serena as the star.

Instead, he was going to let himself do something he almost never allowed himself to do. And it didn't involve sex. Or tattoos. Or heavy drinking.

He was going to put his thoughts on hold and allow himself to fall asleep in his chair. With his cat. And hope to hell that when he woke up, a solution had magically slid into his skull and made itself known.

Seriously?

He was pretty sure all that was going to happen was that he'd wake up cranky and sore and wishing he'd taken the time to stretch out in his own bed.

But it was what it was. And for tonight, he was going to be okay with it staying like that.

* * *

For a brief second after she hoisted herself out of bed and her feet touched the ground, the world spun at a crazy angle. It righted itself almost immediately, but it startled her. She blinked and stood there with an outstretched hand, waiting for the sensation to come again.

It had to be that crazy dream.

That stupid strobe light at the bar from Cozumel had visited her last night. And not in an erotic, sexy way either. Not that that would have been any better. No. She'd been running for her life. Fleeing from something that was just behind her but that remained unseen. Every time she'd turned to look, nothing was there but a shadow.

She blew out a breath and let herself take a tentative step toward her bathroom.

Still steady.

Okay—that's all it had been. The remnants of a nightmare she was glad was over. Time to get ready for work.

A sense of anticipation slid over her that hadn't been there yesterday. Maybe because the reality of working with Toby hadn't been quite as traumatic as it could have been.

He was just a regular guy. Right? One that was crazy sexy and a little intense, but a lot of surgeons were like that. It also explained the precision in the way he'd kept her on the razor edge of climax in Cozumel. Time and time again, he'd brought her almost there only to pull back at the last minute. A shiver of heat went through her.

Oh, God.

She could hear Avery, her roommate, in the kitchen. Cutlery was clanging, and it gave her a sense of normalcy. Serena had needed someone to help split expenses in nursing school, and finding him had been a godsend. They got along like a dream, in a purely platonic way, which had helped her survive the frantic pace of school. They'd each known when to tiptoe around the other, and Serena had poured her heart out to him one time when she'd been so frustrated with one of her courses that she'd considered dropping out of the program. He'd talked her down from the ledge, and for that she owed him a huge debt of gratitude. Because she was finally where she needed to be.

Avery had had a secret of his own that he'd wanted kept from the school, and especially Paz Memorial, where he also worked. He didn't want any special favors or treatment. And Serena respected the hell out of him for that.

Grabbing a quick shower, she toweled off and got dressed, putting a quick coating of mascara on her lashes and dabbing some clear lip balm on her mouth. She let her hair down from the clip and allowed the waves to fall around her face. The humid days of summer made it impractical to try to straighten the thick tresses. They would just go back to their crazy, untamed state. Her ex, Parker, had said the thing he loved most about her was her hair.

She didn't get it. At all. But because of how strong his personality had been, she'd found herself subconsciously trying to please him until she'd realized with horror that it was becoming a habit. A dangerous one. One that she imagined her mother had once played when dating Serena's dad. For her mom, it had signaled the loss of autonomy and independence. So maintaining her independence was something that was now super important to Serena.

Once she'd realized she was falling into a

vat of complacency with Parker, she'd found herself fighting the curls, straightening and straightening them until she'd worn out her flat iron. She went to the store and stared at a replacement iron for a long time before putting it back on the shelf. It wasn't worth it. *He* wasn't worth it. No one was.

She'd ended the relationship not long after that. She wasn't sure why, except that she didn't want to be with someone who'd made her feel she had to fight to maintain her sense of self. Parker hadn't meant to make her feel that way. But some of the little things he'd said and done had reminded her a little too much of her dad. Hypersensitive? Yes. She could admit it. And until she could figure things out, she didn't need to be in any kind of relationship.

She needed to work on what was most important to her: her career.

Her time with Toby in Cozumel had been perfect in that she now knew she could sleep with someone without feeling forever tied to them. Not that she was going to start clubbing any time soon. But knowing she could cut loose and have fun and then snip whatever thin thread that bound them together and go on her merry way was relieving in a way she didn't quite understand.

But then again, she'd never expected to see the person she'd done that with again. And she was finding it harder to deal with than she'd expected.

Sliding her comfy shoes on, she exited her bedroom and found Avery with a sizzling pan filled with a tantalizing scent. "What is that?"

"Omelet. There's more than enough to share."

Her nose twitched, feeling slightly guilty. "Are you sure?"

"Positive. Besides, I've barely seen you all week. It'll be good to have a few minutes doing something normal. Something that isn't life-or-death."

"I agree." She dropped into a chair and watched as he used a spatula to divide the eggs and slid her half onto a plate. "Tell me I shouldn't expect you to do this every day. Despite the fact that I may or may not have heard someone call you Mr. Sunshine at work."

He made a face. "Yeah, I have no idea where that came from. And don't worry."

He motioned to the skillet. "I don't even do this for *me* every day.

"I hear you. I take it cardiac care is as crazy busy as we are on the surgical floor?"

"Let's see." Avery swallowed his first bite of egg. "Do you sit down for meals?"

"Not so far. You?"

"Same."

She blew out a breath. That was why Paz Memorial was such a popular hospital. It had an impeccable reputation for top-quality care. "How's it going, other than that?"

He stared at his plate for a minute before glancing back up at her with a shrug. "Okay. A couple of bumps in the road, but nothing I can't handle. You?"

"A couple of bumps for me too." She started to echo his thought that it wasn't anything she couldn't handle, but in truth, she wasn't sure yet. She'd hoped at some point to transfer to the ICU after getting her nursing legs under her. But so far, she'd loved her time on the surgical floor more than she'd expected. Whether she was still just in the honeymoon phase of the job or if it was love at first sight, she wasn't sure. But having Toby working there too threw a kink in the works. A big one.

She was about halfway through devouring her breakfast when her jaws quit moving. That weird sensation spiraled through her again, this time with a hint of something crawling through her belly.

"Hey, are you okay?"

She started chewing again as the elusive feeling vanished. "Yeah. Just tired."

He dropped his fork onto his now empty plate. "You have a day off coming up, don't you? Make sure you sleep in."

"I plan to."

He took his plate to the sink and started to rinse it for the dishwasher. "Leave it, Avery," Serena said. "You cooked, so the least I can do is load them in. Besides, I don't have to be at work for another hour."

And in truth, it would keep her from thinking too much about things…or Toby. Avery was right. They were just bumps in the road. Once she got past them, surely things would smooth out, and she'd find herself in a routine. In the meantime, she'd make sure she didn't give off any hints that their night in Cozumel was still hovering in her head.

She definitely wasn't going to lapse into Spanish around him, since he'd seemed to like it when she'd done it that night. She didn't do it nearly as much anymore, anyway. And she didn't really see any reason why she would, unless she had to translate for a patient at some point. So far, no one had asked her to.

"Are you sure you don't mind?"

Her roommate's voice pulled her from her thoughts. "Yep. It's kind of nice to do something that doesn't require quick thinking."

"I get it. Okay, I'm off then. See you."

"Yep. Have a good day. And don't speed over those bumps."

"I don't plan on it."

He closed the front door with a soft click, and she could hear his key locking it behind him.

She got up gingerly, hoping she wasn't coming down with something. That was all she needed. But nothing happened. She felt fine and the omelet had actually been delicious. Piling all of the dishes in the sink, she gave them a quick rinse and stacked them in the dishwasher. She'd just finished when her cell phone went off. Glancing at the readout and hoping it wasn't the hospital already, she relaxed when she saw it was her mom.

"Hola, Mamá. Cómo estás?"

Listening with one ear while her mom recounted her research trip to Greece, she found herself smiling. She was in the planning stages of her latest book, and Serena loved hearing her talk about it. The passion in her voice was evident, and Serena could picture the shine in her eyes, the way she would twirl her hair around one of her fingers, something Serena did as well.

Fifteen minutes later, the call ended. Not because they didn't have anything left to talk about, but because this had grown to be their pattern. They chatted most days. Her mom knew how busy her life had gotten since she'd started nursing school and said she didn't want to monopolize her time. She never did. But her mom had always been someone who showed she cared by subsuming her own wants and needs and taking care of others. It was the one thing that she and

Serena actually argued about. But at least she was living her life fully now. So it was hard to argue with that.

Sliding her cell phone in her pocket, she grabbed her keys and followed the path Avery had taken forty-five minutes earlier. She hoped today would be a good day. She *needed* it to be a good day.

He was struggling.

The patient's husband was trying to explain something to him, but Toby's Spanish wasn't the greatest. Especially when the other person seemed to be talking at a hundred miles an hour. The unconscious woman had come through the emergency department and had been sent straight back to surgery after a knife she'd been using to pry frozen fish apart had slipped and sliced open her arm, cutting through skin and muscle alike. He wasn't sure if she'd passed out from the sight of her own blood or if she had some kind of preexisting condition.

He was waiting on the hospital translator, who was currently helping someone else. If she didn't get here soon, Toby was going to have to trust his own instincts and start treatment.

He caught sight of Jacelyn, who was motioning for Serena to come forward. The nurse took a deep breath and moved toward him.

Was she that reluctant to work with him? If so, they were going to need to sit down and hash this out. He couldn't risk patient care just because they had some personal baggage that needed—

"Serena speaks Spanish. Maybe she can help."

Of course. He'd almost forgotten.

Well. No, he hadn't. Some of those little words and phrases she'd murmured so fluidly had slid over him like silk.

Not the time, Toby.

Without addressing him, Serena turned to the man and began talking, nodding and replying in turn before finally turning back to Toby. "His wife was mugged several years ago and stabbed. When she cut herself, he thinks it brought back those terrible memories. For him too. He heard her scream, and by the time he made it to the kitchen, she was on the floor and there was blood everywhere."

That made more sense. "Ask him if she has any medical conditions we should know about."

She repeated the question to him.

The man nodded. *"Lucinda está embarazada."*

That was one phrase he understood. The man's wife was pregnant. He tensed.

"I understood that. Anything else?"

The answer to allergies or other conditions was met with a shake of the man's head. But he evidently asked if the baby was okay.

"Jacelyn, would you mind paging Gary from Obstetrics?"

"I'll do it right now."

He would have asked Serena to do it, but he needed her to stay with him in case he had more questions for the patient. And he was grateful for her help. He glanced at her with real relief sliding through his veins. "Thanks. Seriously."

"You're welcome. Seriously." The tiny smile that played around her lips made him swallow. But at least some of the tension seemed to have left her.

"Can you get him to sign a consent form and explain that we'll have to take her into surgery to repair the arm? It doesn't look like there's nerve or tendon involvement, so it should be straightforward. I just want Gary to take a quick look at her too."

"Is he an OB-GYN?"

"Yes."

Serena turned back to the man, whose name was Pedro, and explained what was happening while Toby placed another layer of gauze on the wound to absorb the bleeding.

Consent forms were signed just as Gary arrived wheeling a portable ultrasound machine. He smiled at Pedro and introduced himself, switching over to Spanish with ease. Toby really did need to put some more effort into learning the language. Pedro and Serena laughed at something the other man said.

It made Toby feel like an outsider. Something that shouldn't bother him, but it did. Maybe because he'd felt that way in his childhood home a lot of the time. His parents probably hadn't realized what they'd done—they probably still didn't, but it had made it all the more attractive to be somewhere other than home.

Lucinda moaned, and her eyelids fluttered. Pedro gripped her uninjured hand and smoothed her hair back from her face, talking to her in low tones. Her eyes found his.

"El bebé?"

Gary said something to her and then pulled the ultrasound machine to the bed and set it up. They soon found the baby's heartbeat, and he reassured both of them that the little guy was still okay. Of course, he had to translate everything back into English for Toby's sake.

But at least everything was normal. They could give her a light sedation, do the repair to her arm without needing to go all the way to general anesthesia. Because of the trauma she'd experienced before, he'd rather not try it with just a local anesthetic.

"Can you assist with the surgery?" he asked Serena. Because of the translation issue, he'd rather keep everything as consistent as possible, and having Serena in the room would help Toby avoid getting messages secondhand. It would be their first time together in surgery. In reality, he hadn't tried to keep her off his cases. They'd just fallen that way.

"Oh… Of course."

But something in her voice didn't sound super thrilled. Which he understood. He was also less than thrilled with the whole situation, but they were going to have to get through it somehow. And it couldn't be any harder than those last days of working with his ex after discovering what she'd done with his best man.

Jacelyn came back over. "Room one is set up for you."

They got her into the room and found that the team was already there waiting for them. Sedation was a breeze, and Toby made sure they knew she was pregnant, as that could sometimes affect choices in medication.

They carefully peeled back the layers of bloody gauze and found a jagged, ugly wound on an arm that looked none too happy about what had happened.

"Let's get this irrigated so I can take a closer look at what needs to be done." He pulled his loupes onto the bridge of his nose. Serena seemed to anticipate what he wanted almost before he asked. He was impressed. Especially since she didn't have nearly the experience of most of the other nurses on the floor.

She was also obviously interested in everything that went on in the room. Another thing that showed everything was still new and fascinating to her. He wished he still had that sense of wonder.

But he also knew that what was fascinating to him was often someone else's heartache, so he tried to keep that in mind whenever he treated a patient. Especially someone like Lucinda. She had a husband who was very worried about her. And she carried some terrible memories inside of her.

"I'm going to stitch in layers," he explained to Serena. "Fortunately, the wound isn't on an area that has a lot of movement. So it should heal pretty well."

The woman's vitals blipping across the screen to his right were steady. Blood pressure was holding.

He sensed more than saw Serena standing there watching him, surgical instruments neatly laid out on the tray in front of her. "If this were a straight-line slice, I might go with deep dermal sutures or use a set-back suture. But because it's jagged and there is a large span between sides, I'm going to use four-zero VICRYL absorbables on the muscle tissue and the same weight nylon on the dermal layers."

Glancing over, he saw her nod. "Got it. I've heard of set-back sutures in class but have never seen it done in real life."

There was a sense of wistfulness in her words that could have been his imagination. Then again, maybe it wasn't.

"How about I call you in if I ever have a case where I'm going to use it?" He had no idea why he'd offered that, other than the fact that he had a lifelong love of learning and teaching others.

"That would be great."

Serena's hair was all pulled up into a surgical cap, but he knew from his time in Mexico that when set free, her curls were lustrous, beautiful things that framed her face. A painter would have found her fascinating. Not just because of her looks. But because of the way her face moved when she talked, highlighting every single one of her emotions.

Like it had that night in Cozumel.

Right now, he sensed a mixture of interest and nerves coming from her that was understandable. But those nerves didn't get the best of her. Her hands were steady, and she followed his requests without hesitation. Under different circumstances, he might have found himself enjoying working with her.

Actually, he was still enjoying it, and that set him on edge.

She was gorgeous, but hell, he did not want to be attracted to her. Not after what had happened with Tanya. She'd already been working at the hospital when Toby had come on board, transferring from a smaller hospital in Lancaster. Back then everything had seemed so easy, uncomplicated...convenient, even. They'd started dating. That had turned into commuting to work together, since their apartments were near each other. Then they'd gotten engaged and moved in together. They'd been in sync about waiting a few years to have children, which had more than suited Toby, who wasn't at all in a rush. At least, they had been for the first couple of months. Then Tanya had mentioned kids unexpectedly at dinner one night while talking about a girlfriend who'd just had a baby. Those mentions had happened more and more frequently until impending fatherhood seemed to play in his head like a litany. At thirty-five, though, she'd pointed out, he was already older than most fathers she knew.

At the time, it had come across as an accusation.

Toby hadn't been completely sure about having kids at all because he wasn't positive, with his own strange, stilted childhood as his only example, that he actually had what it took to nurture anyone. Much less a child. After the argument with Tanya about his age, he'd found himself avoiding those uncomfortable conversations. That had turned into avoiding most conversations with her at all. Especially ones that might trigger talks about having kids.

It was at that point that his best friend—who was also to be his best man—had come to town for a visit and stayed in their spare room. Toby had been in the middle of a complicated case at work, and so Tanya had offered to show Cliff the sights.

Evidently, one thing had led to another, and things had unraveled pretty quickly.

So no. Attracted to a colleague or not, he'd learned from his mistake. And it was honestly a relief to have fatherhood taken off the table for good.

Besides, he had his cat, Porkchop, the one residual of his relationship that he'd kept. That feline was the closest thing to a kid he was likely to have. And it was enough for him.

He pulled his attention back to the procedure at hand and realized Serena was looking at him funny. "Sorry. Did you say something?"

"Nothing important. I asked if you did setback sutures often."

"Not terribly often. But there are situations where I feel they work better for gaping wounds. They take longer to heal, and getting the stitch tension right is important."

A half hour later, they were done, and Lucinda was waking up from her sedation. Her first question was about her baby, and sure enough, Serena had to translate. Her second question was a little harder. She asked if the hospital had a counselor who could help her work through what had happened with the mugging, so that she didn't have the same reaction if, say, her child was cut by something at some point.

"Tell her I'll look into it. If not, I might have a name for her." He handed Lucinda one of his business cards. "Call me later today and I'll let you know."

He'd actually gone and talked to someone right after his breakup with Tanya, and her advice had been to not make any major decisions for the next year. He'd vowed to make it five years instead. He had four years and nine months left to go to make that goal.

Ha! Falling into bed with Serena probably wasn't what his counselor had had in mind. But hopefully, that was a blip that wouldn't be repeated.

He changed the word *hopefully* to one that had a little more oomph to it.

So no. Not hopefully. Definitely.

That night with Serena would *definitely* not be repeated.

CHAPTER THREE

SERENA HAD WORKED two more surgeries with Toby over the next couple of days, and unlike with Lucinda's, where he'd seemed happy to answer her questions and had even offered to let her see a specialized suture procedure, he'd been reserved. Quiet. He answered questions when she asked but didn't offer anything more.

She'd been surprised when he had the name of a counselor on his phone, but she wasn't sure why. She shouldn't be curious about it.

But she was.

She went over to the nurse's desk after checking on a patient to find Toby there talking to Jacelyn. She got there in time to hear the woman say to him, "Just a heads-up, Toby. Tanya stopped by this morning.

Said she was visiting HR to pick up a letter of recommendation." Jacelyn's lips tightened. "She asked about you, Toby."

His eyes met Serena's before moving back to the other nurse. She could have sworn there was a quick flash of guilt in his glance. "Okay, thanks."

That was it. He moved away and headed on his way without another glance in her direction.

Before she could stop herself, she asked, "Who's Tanya?"

It wasn't a totally unprofessional question, right? But what if this woman had been fired because of something Toby had reported her for? In this day and age of mass shootings, it was better to be prepared in case a disgruntled employee decided to seek revenge.

What she wasn't prepared for, however, was Jacelyn's answer.

"Toby's fiancée." Her nose wrinkled in distaste. "I should say ex-fiancée. She cheated on him and ran off with his best man."

Shock went through her. For some reason, she couldn't picture the surgeon being engaged. He seemed totally at home with being single. And he didn't seem the type given to big displays of emotion.

Of course, he'd been different in Mexico. More open. More spontaneous. Maybe that was the side of him that his ex had usually seen.

She couldn't think of anything to say, except for, "How awful."

"Yes. I'm just hoping she hasn't realized her mistake and decided to come sniffing around here again. They were supposed to honeymoon in Mexico."

Mexico.

With a voice filled with dread, she asked. "When was the wedding supposed to be?"

"About a month ago."

A pang of nausea went through her. A month ago. That was when she had found out she'd passed all of her exams and landed the job at Paz Memorial. When she'd gone to Cozumel to celebrate. When she'd met Toby.

God. Had she been a stand-in for this Tanya person? She didn't know why, but the thought filled her with a sense of horror.

"What does Tanya look like?"

"Pretty. Dark hair…a little like yours. But definitely not a nice person."

Somehow, she got through the rest of the conversation, quickly changing the subject to something work related. But that didn't mean her mind had stopped mulling over what she'd just learned.

Had he seen a counselor after his fiancée cheated on him? Was sleeping with Serena his own form of revenge?

Except he would have been more likely to do that under her nose, wouldn't he?

Shake it off, Serena. You won't know for sure unless you ask him.

Yeah, she was never, ever, ever going to do that. Not only because he didn't seem anxious to talk about their night together, but because she might be mortified by his answer. Not that she would have wanted him to express his undying love for her. No. Her climb up the nursing ladder was best done while single. Maybe once she'd been here for a couple of years she might start dating again. That was a big maybe. Right now, marriage and children were kind of nebulous things that she might decide she wanted one day. But not now. Not when she still had so much to learn about herself and her own ambitions.

And if the time came to start a family and she wasn't with anyone? Well, you didn't have to be in a relationship nowadays to have babies.

Thank God.

But it could wait a few more years.

With that thought in mind, she pushed the queasiness of her discovery about Toby out of her head and got back to work.

Jacelyn found her a few minutes later. "Hey. Mabel Tucker is asking to see you."

Their splenectomy patient. "Is she okay?"

"Yep. They're looking to maybe release her earlier than expected since she's been working hard at rehab. She wanted to make sure she saw you before she went home."

"That is great news." Especially since Mabel had not been in good shape when she'd arrived at the hospital. "I'll head over there, if there isn't anything you need me to do before that."

Lucinda would be back on Monday to have her stitches removed. One thing that surprised Serena was how quickly you could get attached to certain patients. She could see why nursing school had needed to drill it into their heads that they had to remain objective.

She was following that protocol in that she wasn't emotional during treatment. But surely it was natural to be happy about positive outcomes, wasn't it? She wasn't sure. But Jacelyn hadn't seemed peeved that a patient had asked for her.

"Nope. Why don't you head to lunch after you've seen her? It's been kind of a crazy morning."

Yes, it had been. She'd assisted with three surgeries since she'd arrived this morning. One appendectomy, a patient who'd come in with a partially amputated foot and a drunk driver with a brain bleed.

It was interesting working with different doctors as well. And seeing so many different types of injuries. But it was also mentally taxing, and she found she was already dragging with exhaustion, and it was barely noon.

"Thanks. I will."

She arrived at Mabel Tucker's room and dredged up a smile before going inside. Her patient was sitting up in bed, the bruising around her eyes starting to turn the slightest bit yellow around the edges, a good sign that there was healing going on just below the surface. "I hear you're getting sprung today.

I'm sorry I didn't make it over sooner. How are you doing?"

"It's okay. And better, actually. The pain meds are finally making some headway."

Serena nodded. "I think your body is doing its part too."

"I hope so. I'm still pretty sore, but I actually told Tom to go back to work today." She laughed. "And then they told me I was going to get to go home, so he'll have to get off early anyway."

"I can't think of any better reason to have to leave work." She moved closer and squeezed Mabel's hand. "I'm so happy for you."

"Me too. We've been talking about… Well, thinking about starting a family. We've been married five years and have been waiting for the perfect time. But after the accident…" Her chin wobbled for a second before she continued. "Is there ever an ideal time? You never know what life is going to throw at you."

"No, you don't." A wave of compassion went through her, not to mention an unexpected pang of longing. Hadn't she just been thinking about her career and how she wanted to get settled before making any kind of decisions about having kids? But what would happen if at each milestone she convinced herself to wait a little longer? And then a little longer after that? Mabel was younger than she was.

Even so, Serena wasn't an old maid, by any means.

"Do you think I'm crazy?" Mabel asked.

"No. Not at all. I always think it's good to evaluate what's important to you at regular intervals."

"Will not having a spleen affect my chances of carrying a baby to term?"

She hesitated. She didn't want to give Mabel incorrect information. "Let me put a quick call in to your surgeon and see if he's available."

Taking out her cell phone, she called Jacelyn. "Is Dr. Renfro in surgery?"

There was a pause. "No, I'm not seeing one listed. Do you need him?"

A moment of shock went through her followed by the realization that the other nurse was only asking if she needed him in a professional sense. God, she needed to get herself together. "I'm here with Mabel Tucker, and she has a question about getting pregnant since she no longer has a spleen."

"Ah, I see. Let me page him. Or you can."

Gah! She didn't want to. Not this soon after starting her job.

"Would you mind? He can call me directly, if he wants to."

"Yep, I will. I'll let you know if he's not available for some reason."

"Thank you."

She hung up and then looked at Mabel. "She's paging him to see if he's available. Has he been in to see you yet today?"

"No. But I assumed maybe before I left he'd come in."

"Yes, I'm sure he will. But it can't hurt just to double-check. He would be the one releasing you, anyway."

Less than a minute later, her phone rang, and she swallowed when she saw the hospital's name displayed. "Serena Dias here."

"Serena, it's Toby. Are you with her now?"

"I am."

"I was headed that way. Be there in a minute."

With that, the line went silent.

Okay, then. She'd gotten no indication of

whether he was peeved that she'd had him tracked down. But then again, he'd made it sound like he'd been on his way, anyway.

He also hadn't told her whether he wanted her to stay there or not, so she was hesitant. But it didn't feel right to just suddenly tell Mabel she was leaving. So she made herself busy, taking vitals to be ready with them in case he asked.

She'd just finished when he pushed through the door. His eyes were on Mabel and not her, although why would he look at her?

He smiled. "You're looking even better than you were yesterday. I was on the fence about releasing you then or today, but I thought you might benefit from another day of being waited on hand and foot."

Mabel laughed. "I'm going to say, your menu could use a little work."

"So I've heard."

He finally acknowledged Serena. "You can reach me on my cell anytime, you know."

That made her gulp.

"Okay, thanks. Mabel was asking about pregnancy following a splenectomy."

He sat on the stool and wheeled himself

over to the bed. "You should be able to get pregnant, but we would want to follow you carefully. There are some elevated risks, but most of them can be managed." He paused. "We definitely would like you to receive some additional immunizations for pneumonia and flu fairly soon."

He talked to her about the spleen acting as a filter for the vascular system to catch microbes and debris before things could spiral out of control. "The liver will take over some of the spleen's duties. But we still worry about infections."

"For how long?"

"You'll have to keep on top of it for the rest of your life."

Mabel seemed to sink deeper into her pillow. "Better that than the alternative, right?"

"That's my thinking. I want you to know I would not have removed your spleen unless I thought it was absolutely necessary for saving your life."

"I know that. And I appreciate it. I'll do whatever I need to do. But I can get pregnant?"

"I don't see any reason why not. I'd like to get our OB-GYN in on the conversation, though, before you make any of those decisions. Would you like to talk to him before you're released?"

She nodded. "Yes, please. I'd prefer to wait until Tom gets here, though. I want him to hear whatever the other doctor has to say."

"I completely understand. I'll arrange for a consult. If there's a problem with getting it before you're released, I'll make sure he's available when you come back in for a recheck. Does that help?"

"Yes, thank you."

"I'll get back to you as soon as I hear from him. Can I check you over while I'm here?"

"Of course."

Toby was just as thorough with this evaluation as he'd been with that first postsurgical exam. When he finished he said, "Everything looks great. You're a model patient. We're going to try to keep you headed in that direction."

"I can't thank you enough. You saved my life."

"Believe it or not, you had a lot to do with that. You're young and strong and your body was fighting hard to keep you alive until the EMTs got you to the hospital."

He might have been brusque with Serena on the phone, but his bedside manner was actually pretty damned outstanding. He was direct rather than patronizing, but he wasn't impatient. And he was an excellent surgeon. If she had to have surgery, she would trust him implicitly.

"Before you're actually released, I'll come in and go over everything later this afternoon. And I'll want to see you in a couple of days to get your sutures out. I don't want you around a lot of people until you've had a chance to have some booster shots. And unfortunately, you'll need to wear a medical alert bracelet for the rest of your life to let first responders know you've had your spleen out."

"Wow. And all of this because of a drunk driver."

"I know. I'm sorry." He gave her hand a quick squeeze. "Don't hesitate to let Serena or one of the other nurses know if you or your husband have any other questions before I come back."

"Thank you again."

"You're very welcome."

Serena nodded to him and waited a minute or two after he left before saying her own goodbye to Mabel. Not because she was afraid to be around him, but just because she didn't want to look like she was angling for some extra chitchat.

Once out of the room, she headed for the hospital cafeteria, opting for a sandwich and salad and then deciding she wanted to eat outside in the garden area of the hospital rather than being stuck inside.

As soon as she stepped into the heat of the outdoors, she breathed a sigh of relief. While she liked air conditioning as well as anyone, it was always nice to be out in what she called "real air" for a while. Especially since it was so chilly inside sometimes.

The clay-tiled area had lush greenery meandering down the center of the space, and various concrete tables and benches were scattered around the open areas. Her eyes traveled the perimeter for a second before stopping dead.

Okay, she hadn't expected Toby to be out here. He had a cup of coffee and was looking at something on his phone. She started to take a step backward, thinking maybe she'd go back inside after all. Except right at that exact moment, as if sensing some kind of movement, his eyes came up and caught her midstep. He looked at her for a moment.

"Want to join me?" His low voice carried across the empty space.

What could she say? No? That would seem rather rude at this point, since it was obvious she was on her lunch break.

So she forced her legs to move toward his table and lowered herself onto the bench across from him. She really didn't want to have to eat in front of him. For some reason, she was suddenly self-conscious. She didn't like it at all.

Shades of her time with Parker.

So she tilted her chin and pulled back the cellophane cover on her egg salad sandwich.

She could feel him watching her for a second before he said, "Most people don't venture out here this time of year. They can't take the heat."

Serena swallowed. Right now, she was having a little trouble taking the heat too. But it was more from the heat generated from the churning of her innards rather than the balmy air. "I'm from Mexico, so it kind of feels like home to me."

Damn. She hadn't meant to mention her home country in front of him. It wasn't that she was trying to hide where she was from—after all, he knew that. It was more like she was trying to hide from what their time together had been like while there. She also didn't want him to know that Jacelyn had told her why he'd been in Mexico that fateful day.

"Yes. The heat there was…unexpected."

His words drove the breath from her lungs. She stared at him. When he tilted his head with a frown, she realized he was talking about the temperature and not their night together.

Dios. She needed to be careful. The last thing she wanted was for him to figure out that everything he said was viewed through the filter of that one hot, passionate night they'd spent together. Especially when something inside of her was whispering to her that she could have that again, if she just let herself.

No. It wasn't smart to even let herself think that way. And just because she was looking through some distorted filter, that didn't mean that he had the same view. In fact, it was pretty obvious he didn't. Instead, she was seeing special inflections in his words that weren't there. Like the ones about the heat being unexpected.

She took a bite of her sandwich and swallowed before changing the subject completely. "Mrs. Tucker seems to be taking everything remarkably well."

"Yes. Maybe a little too well. Used to be that a splenectomy was done a lot more than it is now. But we've discovered that removing the spleen brings a whole set of complications with it."

"I actually did some more reading on it, since it's the first case I've been involved with that's had one."

"And what did your research say?"

Was he being sarcastic for how she'd turned to Dr. Google? She searched his face but found only genuine curiosity.

"I didn't think to look for pregnancy-related issues, but I did find that there's a much higher chance of vascular events like blood clots in those with a splenectomy, and like you'd said, the risk of serious illness. And that some people actually have a second spleen that can take over if the first one is injured."

"I'm impressed. Unfortunately, Mabel isn't one of the ones with an accessory spleen."

"I figured you would have said something to her if she were." Serena realized her elbows were on the table and that she'd leaned toward him as she was speaking. She made a conscious move to sit back and took another bite to prevent herself from running away with another tidbit from her research.

"She will need to be monitored for a while, and she needs to make all of her doctors aware that she's had her spleen removed. But other than that, with some care, she can lead a normal life. Have kids. *If* that's what she really wants to do."

Her brows went up. "You say that as if having children would be something bad."

"Not bad. No. It's just not for everyone."

He made it sound like he was one of those people. Had he and Tanya disagreed on having children?

"Are you talking in general terms? Or personal ones?" Why had she asked that? It was really none of her business.

"Mostly general. But I don't really see children in my future either. You?"

Touché, Dr. Renfro.

She'd had no business asking him anything so personal. He had every right to turn it back around on her.

"I think I might like kids at some point, yes. Although not for a while. And I'm thinking that maybe it's something I'd rather do on my own. Relationships are…complicated."

Putting his coffee cup to his lips, he drank before setting the empty cup back on the table. "That they are. Whether they're years long or only last a single night. Kind of like Mabel's splenectomy, they bring with them their own list of repercussions."

This time, there was no doubt he was talking about their time in Cozumel. They stared across the table at each other.

She bit her lip. The man really was very attractive. With his electric-blue eyes, and stubbled jaw, she could imagine he got second glances wherever he went. But it wasn't just his looks. It was something inside of him that superseded his physical attributes. It was a dangerous combination.

He could probably have a new hookup or

date every week if he wanted one. Except it appeared that he agreed with her that involvements weren't the simple things they were made out to be.

Before she had a chance to comment back, he glanced away and stood. "Well, I should get back. I've spent longer out here than I should."

Spent too long eating lunch? Or with her?

But there was no way she was going to ask. So she nodded and said, "Thanks for letting me join you."

"Not a problem."

But she felt like it was, and she wasn't sure what to do about it.

He headed for the door, and she knew this particular conversation was a closed book. And she, for one, didn't want to reopen it, because she would twist his words one way and then another, trying to find some hidden meaning in them. Even as she thought it, her stomach clenched, and the egg salad she'd just eaten gathered at the bottom of it, forming a rock. A kind of queasy, greasy rock that never quite stayed still, reminding her of that feeling of unsteadiness she'd felt over the last several days.

For the second or third time, she hoped she wasn't coming down with something.

But whatever it was, from now on she was going to avoid personal subjects with her co-workers whenever possible.

And especially with one Tobias Renfro.

CHAPTER FOUR

TOBY WASN'T SURE how the subject of children or relationships had come up, but they were definitely not things he wanted to tackle. With anyone.

Especially not someone he'd slept with. It made him uneasy in a weird kind of way. He was sure Serena wasn't angling for anything; it had just been an innocent conversation she might have had with anyone, but for some reason it had struck a raw nerve. Maybe because of Tanya showing up unexpectedly, followed by Mabel asking about getting pregnant.

They said things came in threes, didn't they? Well, as long as the whole pregnancy thing didn't come after him, it didn't matter.

He'd used protection when they were together. In fact, when they'd crashed into that hotel room and fallen onto the bed, she'd specifically asked if he had some. So he was pretty sure she wouldn't have asked if she'd been planning on using him as some kind of sperm donor. Although she had mentioned wanting to go it on her own when she eventually did have kids.

Ridiculous. She'd *asked* him to use a condom, which he'd already planned on doing.

But he could see how if a woman wanted to have a baby and didn't want a relationship, that was one easy way to get what you wanted. Except Toby would never be irresponsible enough to not use protection. Unless she asked him not to and said she'd taken care of it. And probably not even then. Because he didn't believe in shirking his responsibilities. If he got someone pregnant, and the woman chose to carry the pregnancy to term, he would feel obligated to provide in some way for that child.

Obligated to provide…

Something in his gut roiled in protest. He could envision his parents saying something very similar to one another. Although they'd never voiced that in front of him. But providing for his physical needs had seemed to be paramount on their list of things to do for their child. Emotional needs, not so much. Even now that he was an adult, there were no chatty phone calls. Just birthday cards and the perfunctory call at Christmas.

And if his attitude really was all about obligations like theirs was, he couldn't envision himself having anything positive to add to a child's life.

He brooded over it in his office for a half hour after he'd shared that table with Serena before finally switching off those thoughts. Not that it was an easy task. It seemed everything was coming up babies right now.

And then, there was Tanya. Why come to the hospital in person? And why was she suddenly looking for a letter of recommendation? Was she not happy with her life in San Francisco? Her life with Cliff? Hell, he hoped she was, hoped she didn't have any ideas of trying to get back together with him, because that had ended the second she'd confessed that she'd slept with his best friend. His love had died a quick, hard death—actually, it had been on life support even before that moment. No extraordinary measures would bring it back to life now.

The arguments over children and his eventual regrets over getting engaged to her in the first place just added to that sense of his not having what it took to sustain a relationship. Like there was some personality flaw that wouldn't allow him to form lasting emotional attachments. Did he really want to raise a child, if so? Did he want to parent a baby the way he'd been parented?

No.

But it was a moot point. Things with Tanya were over. Forever. So hopefully she'd gone back to San Francisco with her letter and that would be the last he ever saw of her.

Right now, he needed to get thoughts of Tanya and Serena out of his head and put his attention back on getting Mabel Tucker's discharge instructions together like he'd promised he would. He would worry about the rest of it later.

And only if it became necessary.

Serena loved Balboa Park. It was one of her favorite spots in all of San Diego. She came here every morning for a yoga class that was held in an area shaded by majestic palm trees. Unrolling her mat, she joined the other people who were already doing some gentle stretching in preparation for the half-hour-long session. She could just as easily do the moves in her apartment, but motivation was the problem. It was easier to find things to clean than to spend time on herself. And there was just something about sharing the experience with others that couldn't be beat.

Their instructor, Veronica, had a portable sound system that was just loud enough to be heard over the soothing sounds of a nearby fountain. When the instructor was ready, she took the group through a preplanned series of stretches that started off easy and moved into some of the more difficult poses. The pull of Serena's muscles and tendons as she worked through the routine felt good. She'd been wound up tight this week, and her stomach was still somewhat messed up. She'd thrown some menstrual products in her bag, thinking maybe that was part of her problem, although she'd never been particularly regular.

They got through the hardest portion of the routine and then entered a cooldown phase. She never had time to run back by the apartment afterward, but the park was close to the hospital, so she would just wear her yoga pants and T-shirt and walk to work, switching to her scrubs in the staff changing area.

Feeling more rejuvenated than she had felt for the last two weeks, she determined today was going to be a better day. She had the power to shape her attitude, and today she was going to try not to let anything get to her. Including Tobias Renfro. Her encounter with him at lunch had been unsettling, to say the least. One minute he was talking about not wanting kids, and the next he was making a veiled reference to their night together. Unless she was reading more into his words than the situation warranted. Which was a very real possibility. As was the worry that she might be developing an unhealthy obsession with the man.

The class ended, and she rolled her mat back up, tucking it into the beach bag she'd brought with her. She exchanged some small talk with a couple of regulars to the class and then headed on her way, taking one of the main paths, staying to the side so runners could get past her.

She had a spring in her step that she allowed to remain as she took in the beauty of the park. Although she'd relocated to the city to go to nursing school, she'd fallen in love with San Diego and had decided to stay here. She was glad she had. This place had it all. Beaches, parks and a great nightlife. And she wouldn't trade her friendship with Avery for anything.

He'd been a big part of her life for the last several years, and although their schedules were a little different now than they'd been during their classes and they saw less of each other, she knew she could tell her friend anything and it wouldn't go any further. Although she hadn't told him about that night in Cozumel yet. Not because she was embarrassed about it, but it was just nice to have a tiny area of her life that no one knew about other than her. And there'd been no real reason to tell him.

She'd been doubly glad she hadn't told him when she realized she'd be working with the very person she'd slept with.

Maybe she needed to get back on birth control. Fortunately, Toby had taken care of that aspect of their being together that night, and she would never have unprotected sex, but it wouldn't hurt to have an IUD put in as an extra safeguard. The pill had not been her friend when she and Parker were together, but he hadn't been interested in taking on any of that part of their relationship. In fact, she halfway got the feeling that he would have been happy if she'd gotten pregnant. The better to control her with? More and more, as she looked back at that relationship, she realized she'd probably dodged a bullet. There'd been warning signs that she'd probably ignored, thinking she was overreacting. But the last straw had been his intimation that he'd rather she not be as dedicated to her career path as she'd been. It's probably what had happened with Mom and Dad.

Heavens, she hadn't thought about Parker in a while. And as soon as she'd broken up with him and left their apartment, she'd put an ad up looking for a new place so she wouldn't be tempted to go back to him. When Avery had immediately responded offering a room at his place, she'd initially been hesitant about sharing a space with another man. But he'd quickly put her at ease, and she hadn't regretted the decision for even an instant.

She was so lost in her thoughts that when

a jogger pulled up beside her, it took her a second to realize they'd altered their pace on purpose. Glancing to the side to see Toby, she closed her eyes for a quick second. So much for the resetting that her yoga class had done.

Toby was dressed in running gear, and sweat streamed down his temples and darkened the chest of his gray T-shirt. The sleeves of the tee had been cut off and showed off his tanned arms and the curve of his biceps.

Ugh! He was even more gorgeous when he was hot and sweaty than he was in his casual hospital clothes. The word *steamy* took on a whole new meaning.

She gritted her teeth, managing to get out, "I didn't know you ran in the park."

What else could she say? It was true. And if she had known, she might have been a little less inclined to do her yoga classes here.

No. She was not going to do that. Not going to change her routine just to make it more convenient for him to run here.

Except he hadn't asked her to. She was being ridiculous!

"And I didn't know you…walked here?"

That made her smile. He'd had no idea

what she'd been doing here. "Yoga. They teach classes here."

"Ah. I see."

But she didn't think he did, and she felt a little defensive. "It's a bit harder than it sounds."

"I wasn't saying it's not. I just didn't realize they had yoga classes in the park."

"You should try it sometime. Several of the people that come use it to warm up before running."

Her mouth snapped shut. Why on earth had she said that? The last thing she wanted was for Toby to show up at one of her classes and disrupt her chi.

"Seriously?"

Okay, now that was the last straw. "Yes, seriously. You should try it before you laugh something off."

He frowned. "I actually wasn't laughing it off. I just didn't know that runners often used that technique. When are your classes?"

Wow, she was taking everything he said and twisting it into something negative. And she wasn't quite sure why.

"They're every day at 6 a.m."

Maybe she'd jumped to conclusions because he made her, well, jumpy. And because Parker had pooh-poohed yoga as being nothing but fluff. And because of that, she'd basically just taunted Toby into taking one of her classes.

Parker had seemed so charming and accommodating at first. After a month of dating, he'd encouraged her to move in with him, saying it would help both of them with expenses. But once she was installed in the apartment, his demeanor had changed subtly. Good-natured coaxing had shifted to guilting her into things. Including sex. By the time she recognized that she was falling into the same patterns as her mom had with her dad, they'd been together almost six months. The relationship had become stifling, and she'd known she had to break it off.

It was easy to paint anyone with alpha characteristics with the same brush, but she knew it wasn't fair to do so. Toby had stood up to the creep at the bar, but he hadn't pressured her to do anything. In fact, if she'd shunned his help, she had no doubts that he would have backed off immediately. He was a leader. But he didn't turn that natural ability into an abuse of power. It was why everyone she'd met so far respected him.

Actually, she did too, if she were honest with herself.

What harm could it do if he joined her class? Maybe it would help her see another side of him that would make her respect him even more.

Was that such a good idea, though? Couldn't respect turn into other things?

Not if she didn't let it.

"How long are the sessions, and is this okay to wear?" Toby held his arms out as if to let her look at his attire. And she did. But it also gave her a reason to remember exactly what that body had looked like without any clothing at all. The side of her breast tingled as a memory swept over her, and she pressed her arm hard against the area to keep the sensation from spreading. Her malleable bra was great for yoga, but not so great when it came to hiding erect nipples.

"It's fine." She jerked her eyes away from him. "Classes are a half hour. Most runners just wear whatever they're going to run in afterward."

"But you don't."

"Sorry?" She shifted her glance back to him.

"You don't run afterward?"

"No. I mean, I've competed in a couple of half-marathons, but running tends to be a solitary endeavor, and I like having company. So the yoga classes are perfect."

"What time do you have to be at work tomorrow?"

She blinked. "My shift starts at nine, but I like to go straight there after yoga. It's a short walk and I can change and get my mind where it needs to be before I start my workday."

"I'll tell you what. I'll come to yoga class if you'll come running with me afterward. I can see if yoga works for me. And you can experience running with someone else. It can be a one-time thing, so no one feels pressured to continue."

What? He was asking her to run with him? Why?

Ha! Maybe because she'd suggested he try her class. If she refused, wouldn't she be guilty of exactly what she thought he'd been doing?

"You've got yourself a deal." On impulse, she stuck her hand out to shake on it.

He accepted her offer and gripped her hand. His fingers were cool against her skin, and yet, his touch burned her in a way that said her bra was definitely going to fail her. Sure enough, she felt it happen...

She swallowed and their eyes met. And she could tell he knew. God! He knew exactly what she was feeling.

But he didn't let go. And neither did she. They stood there for a long moment while the skin of her arms prickled as if wanting his palm to slide down them too.

Strands of her hair slid across her cheeks in the warm breeze, just as his gaze dipped to her mouth. It finally woke her up to the fact that she *wanted* him to kiss her. The way that he had in Cozumel.

That would be a total disaster. For both of them.

As if reading her thoughts, he released her hand and turned to walk again. "Well, I have surgery in a half hour. Would you mind if I went ahead and finished my run?"

Mind? No. She'd be relieved. The last thing she wanted was for them to walk the

whole way there or arrive at the hospital together. She was having enough trouble being
around him without worrying about gossip.

"Of course not. Go ahead."

"Okay. See you over there."

"See you."

With that, he began running again, giving her a fantastic view of his strong back
and even stronger glutes, which flexed and
released with each step he took. And since
he couldn't see her staring at him, she drank
in the sight, knowing that was all she was
going to do. Maybe she should call off running with him.

But if he showed up for her class and she
suddenly said, *Sorry, I'm not going with you*,
she'd have to come up with some kind of excuse that didn't include phrases like, *Would
you like to fall into bed in a sweaty heap
with me after this?* Or, *Hey, want to share a
shower stall?*

Ugh. That was what had gotten her into
this mess in the first place. Letting her id go
wild that night in the club.

It only went to show you that letting your
impulses run amok was not such a good idea.

But at least it hadn't been her suggestion

that they exercise together. Or had it? She'd kind of been the one to get that ball rolling. And now it was racing down the hill and probably getting ready to smash against the nearest obstacle.

God, those thoughts were starting to whip her stomach into a frenzy again. It had been a week, and she'd had no other symptoms, so it was doubtful she was catching a cold or the flu or even COVID-19. So what else could it be?

Nerves?

Her period getting ready to start?

How long before Cozumel had she had her period? Maybe a couple of weeks? She didn't tend to track it because of how inconsistent her cycle was. So, two weeks before Cozumel. Then four weeks had passed before she'd started at the hospital. And she'd been at Paz Memorial just over two weeks, so she did some quick addition… Two plus four plus two equaled—eight.

Eight weeks since her last cycle. Had she ever been that late before?

She didn't think so. Five or six? Yes. That happened all the time. But eight?

The products in her bag seemed to taunt her. She'd slept with Toby six weeks ago.

No, no, no...

It couldn't be that. It would be unimaginable. Horrifying, even. She hadn't gotten pregnant with Parker the whole time they'd been together. There'd never even been the slightest hint that she might be. And she'd never worried much about it, because her irregular cycles had always been *normal*. She'd always taken care of protection, and since they were exclusive and clean, Parker hadn't used a condom. Hadn't wanted to.

But Toby had. There was no way he would have purposely done something to put her at risk. Especially not after his comment about kids.

A trickle of panic went through her. She didn't think she'd ever gone eight weeks without having a period.

She stopped at the entrance to the park as her legs started shaking and her chi deserted her completely. Making her way to the nearest bench, she lowered herself onto it and bent forward, taking slow, deep breaths. Partly to control the sudden nausea that threatened to overwhelm her and partly to slow her racing heart.

How on earth was she going to face Toby at work today? Or, worse, tomorrow morning, when he showed up for yoga class?

She needed to do a pregnancy test to put her mind at ease. But not tonight. Not when she knew she was going to have to speak to him tomorrow morning. He'd see the truth on her face.

Wasn't he going to see it anyway, though?

"Okay, okay. Think about it for a second, Serena," she muttered to herself. "He doesn't have to know about any of this. Even if it turns out you are pregnant, you could let him go on not knowing he'd fathered a child."

Could she do that? Was it even moral to do that? Was she stupid enough to think he wouldn't figure it out?

She didn't know anything. Right now, all she could do was sit here on a park bench and breathe and breathe and breathe.

CHAPTER FIVE

SERENA STARED AT the little stick on the counter the following morning, unable to tear her eyes away as a hundred fears swirled around her, gathering more friends as they went. Pregnant.

She stared at herself in the mirror. How could she be pregnant? It had only been one time. One. Time.

How many women had asked themselves this very same thing? One time was all it took.

Except, they'd taken precautions.

But she knew even the best contraceptives failed from time to time.

After all the times she and Parker had been together, it still made no sense to her that a one-night stand had made the unthinkable happen.

She tore her eyes away from the test results that now seemed to be swaying from side to side and bent over to lay her head on the cool granite countertop. Toby had mentioned that even one night could have repercussions. But she'd never even dreamed that this could be one of them.

She could get rid of it. He'd never know. Never *need* to know. Her fight-or-flight instincts were telling her to run from the situation as far and as fast as she could.

Gulping back a renewed sense of nausea and wondering how in the world she was going to face Toby later that morning at that damned yoga class, she forced herself to shower and get dressed as if it were any other day.

Only it wasn't. But she couldn't hide out in her bathroom forever. Avery was waiting in the other room to hear what the test had revealed. And if she thought it was hard going out there and admitting she was pregnant to him, she could only imagine what it would be like to tell Toby.

She wasn't sure she could do it.

But she had to move. Do something. Maybe her roommate would have some nugget of wisdom that would break through the ice that was beginning to thicken the blood in her veins.

Taking a deep breath and leaving the test on the counter of her ensuite, she opened the door and headed out of her bedroom.

Avery searched her face for a minute before saving her the trouble of getting the word past the lump in her throat. "It was positive, wasn't it?"

Serena nodded and dropped onto the chair across from where Avery sat on the sofa. She'd come home with a pregnancy test last night and told him her fears, leaving out the *who* and *where* of the situation. She'd wanted to do the test right then and there, but he'd convinced her to wait until morning when it would be most accurate. And even though he didn't need to be at work until nine, he'd gotten up at the crack of dawn to hear the results.

"It was. What a nightmare." Even Mr. Sunshine couldn't make her see the positive side of this situation.

"I'm not going to ask you if you're sure, because there's no way in hell you haven't been staring at that stick in shock for the last fifteen minutes. What are you going to do?"

"I have no idea."

"You know who the father is, though."

She gave a choked laugh. She guessed someone at the hospital was going to know about her time with Toby after all. But Avery would keep her secret. Just like she'd kept his.

"Would you believe me if I told you I spent a wild night in Cozumel with one of the trauma surgeons at the hospital?"

"Reginald Miller?" One corner of his mouth curved up in a way that made her burst out laughing.

Maybe Avery could work his magic after all. Dr. Miller was sixty-five and was due to retire in a few months.

"Jerk. Not that Dr. Miller isn't a silver fox. But no, it's not him. It's Toby Renfro."

"Whoa. I never saw that coming."

"I know. I met him in the park yesterday morning and basically accused him of being too macho to participate in my yoga class."

He propped an ankle on his knee. "Not a smart move, Dias."

Avery called her by her last name most

of the time. And Serena liked it. It kind of sealed their friendship.

"I know that. Now. But I wasn't thinking clearly. And I think I see the reason for that now. When it's too late."

It also explained why she'd felt off balance a couple of times when standing quickly and why her stomach had been so wonky the last couple of weeks.

"Are you going to tell him?"

"I don't know if I can. He as much as said he doesn't want kids."

"Really?"

She shook her head. "He told me over lunch when we were talking about a splenectomy patient we'd had who now wants to get pregnant that he didn't see children in his future."

"Sometimes people change their mind."

She squinched her nose at him. "I can't really see him doing that." She twirled a strand of hair around her finger as a renewed feeling of despair went through her.

"In the end, it doesn't matter what he wants or what he doesn't. What do *you* want?"

She twirled her thoughts like she'd done her hair. She knew what she *could* do. What she probably *ought* to do. But what if this was a sign from the universe that now was the time to do this? Mabel Tucker's words came back to her.

Is there ever an ideal time? You never know what life is going to throw at you.

It was very true. Serena didn't see herself putting her career or life on hold in order to have a child. But she'd toyed with eventually including a pregnancy in her life. She wouldn't necessarily have to halt everything for nine months or more. She could work almost up to her due date and then take six weeks off work after she'd given birth.

And then what? How was she going to support them both on her salary? What would she do for childcare when she was at work?

She swallowed. But wouldn't she always wonder those things? She'd already told Toby this might well be something she did on her own.

But how likely was it that she was going to run to the nearest fertility clinic and start the complicated process of artificial insemination or in vitro?

She was already pregnant. Couldn't she

somehow make it work? Single mothers did all the time.

And she respected Toby. A lot. There were worse things out there than having a child that would remind her of a fun time in her life. A time of crazy, once-in-a-lifetime spontaneity.

She finally responded to Avery's question. "I think I'm going to have this baby."

There was a long pause while he studied her face before smiling. "I think you are too. Congratulations. You're going to be a great mom."

"I sure hope so." Serena blew out a breath as the reality of the situation swept over her. "Keep this just between us for now, okay?"

"No worries on that front. I would never betray your trust."

"I know you wouldn't." She bit her lip before asking the question running through her mind. "If you were Toby... Would you want to know?"

He sighed and let his foot slide back to the floor, leaning forward in his seat. "I'm not Toby, though. And I'm not you, so I can't tell you what to do. But if it *were* me... Yes, I'd want to know."

"Even after saying you didn't want to have kids?"

Avery nodded. "That's a hard one. Maybe he'll make it easy and say he doesn't want to be involved."

"And maybe he'll ask me to get an abortion."

"Do you really think he'd do that?"

She thought about it for a minute. "No, I don't." That was the problem. But she could see him secretly wishing she'd get one, though. And since part of the baby's DNA would be his, would it be right to have it even if she knew it was against his wishes?

She had no idea. But what she did think was that Avery was absolutely right. Toby did have a right to know and decide for himself what he wanted to do about it. Should she tell him after the yoga class today? Just thinking about that made her put the back of her hand to her mouth to hold back the sensation of nausea.

She'd have to see if there was an opening to say something. The last thing she wanted to do was blurt it out without having a chance to measure her words.

Maybe he would just do what Avery said

and leave it all to her. She already knew she wouldn't challenge him or ask him for any kind of support. Having this baby was all her decision. And she was perfectly willing to shoulder all the consequences of that decision.

Alone.

Even if it was the hardest thing she'd ever done.

Okay, so Serena was right. Yoga was a lot harder than it looked. Suddenly, he felt every one of his thirty-five years.

But he gritted his teeth and allowed the moves to burn through him. He could see why runners might want to use this before workouts to prevent sports injuries. But he could also see how his pride might force him to push harder than he should to...

Show off?

Hell, no. At least, that shouldn't be his motivation.

He watched Serena out of the corner of her eye as she lay on her stomach and did something the instructor had called the bow pose, bending her legs at the knees while she arched up and caught her ankles with her hands. Hell. He got as far as bending his knees and arching his back, but the whole hand-to-ankle thing? No can do.

"Only do what feels good." The words came from the front of the class. "Your flexibility will increase."

Was she talking to him? He glanced around the area and saw that no, it wasn't just him. Around fifty percent of the group had perfected the move, like Serena, but not everyone. Okay. That made him feel less conspicuous and out of place.

Serena, on the other hand, seemed to have trouble meeting his eyes today.

Was it because of that prolonged handshake yesterday? He hadn't meant that to happen. Had somehow just lost track of where he was. And he'd been pretty sure that in that moment, Serena had too. She'd moistened her lips, and he could have sworn she'd reacted to his touch, although he'd done his damnedest not to let his gaze drift to where he knew that little butterfly lay hidden.

Today, with her sleeveless tank on, he'd caught tantalizing glimpses of it as she'd stretched her body to the side. She probably wasn't even aware that it could be seen. So he'd opted to stare straight ahead and not let his peripheral vision have access to what she was doing. Although it was damned hard.

"Let's move onto our left sides." The instructor's voice was soothing, waiting as they all moved to follow her instructions.

The position had him facing Serena's back. How glad was he that none of the yoga moves had them pairing up?

Very glad. Because even facing this side of Serena was a dangerous proposition. He was very glad when the next set of instructions had them slowly twist their upper torsos until their shoulders were pressed to the ground, arms out to form a T.

There was another pause. "Now turn your head to the right and feel the stretch in your side increase."

And increase it did. But it was a good stretch. And one that was easier than the bow thingamajig.

They switched to the other side and repeated the stretch. Toby closed his eyes and concentrated on what his body was feeling.

This really was nice. He might have to come again sometime. But he wasn't sure he could handle sharing this space every day with Serena. Ever since yesterday, he'd been far too aware of her, moments from their night together sliding through him unexpectedly and putting him off his game. Running would be easier. It was harder to think when you were panting and trying to push through the burn. At least, he hoped it was.

"Okay. Good job, everyone. Lie there until you're ready to get up. No hurry, as always. And hopefully, I'll see you again tomorrow."

Hmm. She'd probably have one less participant tomorrow. He could always find another place where he could do yoga. But how likely was it that it would be at a park where he could run afterward? Serena was right. This really was the best of both worlds.

He got up slowly and waited as Serena did the same. She rolled up the thin mat she'd brought with her. He'd opted to just do the moves directly on the ground. Carrying gear wasn't a great way to run, and he'd left a change of clothes in his locker at work. Serena didn't have the bag with her that she'd had yesterday, but what was she going to do with…? She went up to the instructor and said something to her before handing her the mat. Okay. Well, that was different.

When she got back, he asked, "She's going to hold onto that for you until tomorrow?"

"No, she brings extras that you can borrow for fifty cents. She charges just because it costs her something to sanitize them."

"But yesterday you had your own, didn't you?"

"Yes. But yesterday I wasn't going on a run, like I am today." She seemed to hesitate, chewing a corner of her lip before saying, "Are you ready?"

So despite her kind of quiet attitude this morning, she wasn't bailing on him. "Aren't you going to ask me what I thought of yoga?"

She seemed to relax, as if relieved about something. "Of course. What did you think?"

"Surprisingly, I like it. It's not something I pictured myself doing, but..." He shrugged. "Maybe those are the very things you should try."

She got a funny look on her face, and she stared at him for a long moment before looking away. "And sometimes it depends on what it is."

"Yes. Sometimes." He had no idea what she was talking about, but what else could he say? "Well, you asked if I was ready, so you're up for a run?"

"I'll give it a try. How far are we going?"

"Ten miles?"

When her eyes turned into saucers, he laughed. "I'm kidding. Let's go by time rather than distance. A half hour, say? Same as your yoga class?"

She blew out a breath. "That sounds much more doable for a newbie."

They started out at a slow jog, before she glanced at him. "If you're slowing your pace because of me, don't. I'll tell you if you're going too fast."

And those words transported him right back to Cozumel and her frantically whispered words.

Too fast. God, I don't want this to end. Not yet.

He'd immediately slowed his pace, despite the fact that his body had been screaming at him to end it. To cross that finish line. Except Serena had been right. Delaying their gratification had been so very right.

And had made it that much harder to forget.

Pushing those thoughts to the back of his

head, he picked up the pace and saw her follow right along. He wasn't a sprinter; he preferred to run at a moderate pace. Just enough to let his muscles know they'd been well worked.

Like they'd been that night?

No. Not thinking about that right now.

Ten minutes later, she panted, "Okay, I have a stitch in my side, so I'm going to slow down, but you can keep going."

"Nope." He slowed his footfalls. "You said you didn't like running because you have to do it alone. I'm not going to be the one who makes you do that."

She didn't say anything, and when he glanced over at her, he noticed her arm was draped across her stomach, although she didn't seem to be in distress.

Still… "Hey, are you okay?"

She nodded, still not saying anything, and he swore he saw her chin wobble. He reached out and gripped her wrist, slowing to a stop and pulling her to a halt too. Turning to face her, he touched her cheek. "Serena, what is it?"

A tear slipped free, trickling down her

cheek. He was right. Something was definitely wrong.

"Is it your stomach?"

She closed her eyes, and a squeaked laugh came out. "No. Yes. No."

Okay, that made no sense whatsoever.

"Is it something I can help with?" He used his thumb to wipe away the tear, the moisture pulling at something in his gut.

Her eyes popped open in an instant. "No. Please don't ask me anything else. Not right now. I'm just—trying to absorb some news… There's a decision I need to make."

Okay, so she'd gotten bad news. Or maybe she'd decided something. A thought hit him. "Are you quitting? I know you said not to ask you anything else, but—"

"No, I'm not quitting." She met his gaze. "It has nothing to do with work, I promise. Just something personal."

He studied her for a second before deciding he wasn't going to press her for more answers when it was obvious she didn't want to talk about it. But why had it suddenly been so important to him to know whether or not she was leaving Paz Memorial?

"Got it." He paused. "Well, I hope whatever decision you have to make works out for the best for all involved."

"Yeah. Me too." She released an audible breath. "Do you mind going on without me? Thanks for coming to yoga with me. It's not the running. Or you."

There was a sincerity in her voice that sent a shard through his chest. He wanted to help. But if she wanted him to know whatever it was that had upset her, she would tell him. And although he was loath to leave her standing there, he was pretty sure she wanted to be alone right now, so he took her at her word. "Rain check?"

That made her smile, a look of relief on her face. "You can count on it."

"Okay, see you at work." With those words, he turned and started running again, heading away from Serena and whatever her problem was.

Because really, if she didn't want to tell him, it was none of his business.

Soon, Toby was caught up in his own little world, back to his normal pace that put him in the zone, all the while thinking to himself that Serena might just have been right. That running was better when you had someone next to you.

They had another surgery together that afternoon, and Serena seemed completely recovered from whatever had been wrong this morning. She was professional but not standoffish. "Four-zero nylon suture, please."

She handed him a pre-threaded needle with the perfect amount of suture material running through it. A lacerated liver due to a fall from a ladder had taken some finagling to close, and surgery was already at the three-hour mark. But he wanted to make sure nothing would open up again once he placed the final suture.

Taking his time closing the skin, he kept an eye on the man's blood pressure readings, as any drastic change in it could indicate a complication of both the initial injury and surgery itself. So far, they had held steady, though. He glanced around the room at his team. The people who shared every victory with him. And mourned every loss. He was really lucky to be where he was, with this incredible team. He had never doubted that Paz

Memorial was the place for him. From the moment he'd stepped onto the surgical floor, something had clicked into place. Even that mess with Tanya and Cliff hadn't made him doubt that this was where he belonged, and he'd never been tempted to transfer. Even if Tanya had stayed, he would have somehow figured out a way to work with her. The same way that he and Serena had figured out a way to work together after that initial shock of seeing each other again.

They'd even spent a little time together away from work—not that it was a habit he wanted to get into. Wiping that tear away this morning had forged some kind of emotional bond that he was struggling to break free from. He needed to just keep sawing away at it, no matter how long it took. He still didn't believe that workplace romances were a good idea. For him, anyway. He would never put those rules on anyone else. But he'd seen firsthand the heartache it could cause all involved.

He also knew that he shared a part of the blame for what had happened with Tanya. Her sudden interest in having a child had caused him to pull away from her. Emotional withdrawal seemed to be a remnant of his childhood that had carried over to his adult life. So he was more than surprised by the pull he felt toward Serena. Was it just due to that night in Mexico? Or was it something else? One thing he knew was that he didn't trust himself to hold steady in any relationship.

Giving an internal sigh, he placed the last suture and checked everything once and then again.

"You used set-back sutures."

Her observation startled him for a second.

He looked at the incision line. Yes, he had. He'd done so without thinking. And he was surprised she'd even noticed. Or remembered them talking about that particular technique. He smiled at her. "So I did. I guess you finally got to see them done."

"I'm glad I did. Watching a video isn't quite the same as seeing someone do them live."

"You're right."

The interest and sparkle were back in her eyes, and he found himself glad of it for some weird reason. He didn't want to know her personal problems. But he did like it when someone was excited about their work. It energized him. Made him glad he was a surgeon. Especially on cases like this or like Mabel Tucker when life-or-death situations ended with a good prognosis.

"Speaking of sutures, Mabel Tucker is due to come back into hospital right before five to have her sutures out. Do you want to assist?"

She hesitated, biting her lip. "It kind of depends on how busy my day is. Can I let you know a little closer to the time?"

"Sure."

And just like that, she was back to that quiet, pensive person she'd been during their jog. And he found he wasn't happy with the regression. Despite the fact that she'd said it had nothing to do with him. Well, she'd actually said it had nothing to do with work, not him personally. But since he was part of her work, wasn't it the same thing?

He wasn't quite sure. And now was not the time to ask, especially since she'd been pretty clear about not wanting him to pressure her into talking about whatever it was.

He'd convinced himself he didn't want to know. But now, he was not so sure.

He was sure of one thing, though. It wasn't

just a general sense of malaise. There was a specific reason behind her weepiness of this morning. She'd as much as admitted it.

But unless she wanted to tell him what it was, he was going to have to be satisfied with not knowing.

No matter how hard that might be.

CHAPTER SIX

"DO THEY HAVE these luncheons all the time?"

Serena had spotted Avery across the room at the buffet line and headed over to him, glad to see a familiar face.

One face she hadn't seen here was Toby's. It had been a couple of days since he'd been at her yoga class. He hadn't appeared at the park since then. At least, not that she'd seen. She hadn't even caught sight of him jogging after her class. It made her feel worse somehow. Maybe he was afraid of her having another breakdown like the one during their run.

If it was true and he was avoiding her because of that, how would he react if she told him she was pregnant? God! She didn't even want to think about it.

She hadn't meant to cry. Especially not in

front of him, but when she'd said she needed to slow down and he'd said what he had, it had hit her right in the midsection.

You said you didn't like running because you have to do it alone. I'm not going to be the one who makes you do that.

Emotion had boiled over that had nothing to do with the slight nausea she'd been dealing with at the time. Even now, the memory of the way he'd said that—the way he'd brushed her tear away—had the power to make her to cry all over again.

Because the reality was, she wanted someone there with her. Both during her pregnancy and beyond.

She *didn't* like running on her own. And she actually thought she could raise a baby on her own?

Now Avery was looking at her funny.

"What?"

"I answered your question."

She blew air into her cheeks letting them puff out as she wracked her brain. "Sorry, Ave. What was the question again?"

One of his brows went up. "About the luncheons. And whether they have these all the time?"

She laughed. "Of course. Ugh. My brain isn't quite working like it should be nowadays."

"I've noticed. Any luck with that...decision to tell a certain person something?"

"No. But I'll need to figure it out soon. He's already guessed something is wrong."

Avery's glance went past her before coming back. "Speaking of which. He's here."

There was no need to ask who *he* was. She didn't look. "Any chance I can slide out of here without him noticing?"

"Since he's looking right at us, I would say no."

She glanced up and saw Toby was indeed looking at her. In fact, he'd started heading their way.

"Do you want me to stick around?"

"No, it's okay. Maybe I need to make that decision now."

"Okay, Dias. Good luck. And whatever happens, you'll be okay." He smiled. "Just remember, you're not alone."

"And Mr. Sunshine makes another appearance. I can see why that nickname is gaining traction." Her smile started off bright, but just as suddenly, her eyes watered, and she reached for his hand and squeezed it before going up on tiptoe and kissing his cheek. "Thank you, Avery. You are a good, good friend. The best."

"Don't forget that. I'm here to help."

And then he was gone. Just as Toby arrived. He looked at her for a second. "Someone special?"

"What?"

"The guy you were talking to."

Her brain felt full of cotton wool. "Oh." She glanced at where Avery was already talking to someone else, his ready smile in evidence. "Yes, Avery is pretty special. We went through nursing school together. He's talked me down from a couple of ledges."

His jaw tightened. "I see."

He might, but she sure didn't. He looked almost angry about something. "Is there something you wanted to talk to me about?"

He glanced across the room for a minute toward where Avery had gone before looking back at her. "You forgot to text me about Mabel."

Damn. She had. She'd told him she would check with him when the time got closer. Only she'd forgotten. Or maybe blocked it out in her desperation not to have to talk about anything that didn't have to do with work. Maybe she didn't want to look for an opening to tell him. Maybe that's what it boiled down to.

Maybe she needed to just get this over with.

"You're right. I did. Did she already come by?"

"She did. She's doing really well. She wanted me to let you know that she and Tom have decided to start a family as soon as she's cleared to do so."

It seemed like ages since that talk about timing and how it was never perfect. How crazy was it that Serena had been the one to get pregnant before their patient? And the timing certainly wasn't perfect.

But maybe there was something to what Mabel had said. There would never be a perfect time to get pregnant. Nor would there be a perfect time to tell Toby about the pregnancy. Or not tell him. But one way or the other, she needed to make that decision.

She searched her soul. Could she live with herself for trying to keep him in the dark? For keeping her baby in the dark? If she stayed at Paz Memorial, he was going to put two and two together anyway and would eventually ask her what was going on. And if she left?

Other problems would arise that would be just as hard to deal with.

Her baby would grow up and eventually ask about their father. And it would happen. What would she tell them? She couldn't see a scenario where that question wouldn't arise. And for Toby to have a twenty-year-old young adult appear out of nowhere and say, *Hey Dad, you never knew about me, but I'm your kid.*

She cringed. No. Toby would have every right to hate her for depriving him of his child, or at least for depriving him of the right to decide whether or not he wanted to be involved in that child's life. So leaving Paz Memorial wasn't going to solve her problems. And the truth was, she didn't want to leave.

Realizing he was still standing there looking at her, she blurted out, "That's great about Mabel." She paused. "Hey, can I talk to you? In private?"

"Sure. How about in my office?"

"Perfect. Thank you."

Even though this was her choice, each step felt like it was leading her closer and closer to disaster. Mainly because she had no idea how he was going to react.

But really? It wasn't like she had set out to get pregnant. And she wasn't alone in the getting there.

He bore every bit as much responsibility as she did.

Except he wouldn't be the one ultimately deciding what happened from here. That was all on her. Despite what he'd said during their run, she was alone in that sense. And she alone would bear the consequences for that decision.

They reached his office, and he unlocked the door, letting her go in ahead of him.

Without asking, she locked the door so they wouldn't be interrupted, and then because her legs felt like gelatin, she dropped into the nearest chair and waited for him to round his desk. But he didn't. Instead he pulled out the chair next to hers and sat in it.

He didn't give her a chance to speak first. "I'm feeling a little sucker punched right now, I have to admit."

God! He did not look happy. Had he already figured it out? Or been told by someone? No. The only other person on the planet who knew about the pregnancy was Avery, and there was no way he would have said anything.

She swallowed. "Sucker punched?"

He sat back in his chair and regarded her for a moment before blowing out a rough breath. "I didn't realize you were involved with someone when I met you at the bar in Cozumel."

Shock took all of her thoughts away for a few seconds. "Involved?"

"Serena. Really?"

"I have no idea what you're talking about. If you're referring to that jerk in the bar, I didn't even know him."

His brows came together. "No. Not him. The guy from the luncheon just now. The one you admitted you were involved with."

"I never..." She realized he had taken her words completely out of context. "You mean when I said he was special? He is. But we're not involved romantically. We're roommates. Only roommates. And really good friends."

Her world pieced itself together enough

that a thread of anger came through. "You actually thought I'd sleep with you if I were involved with someone else?"

"It's not like it never happens."

Jacelyn's comments about his fiancée cheating on him came rushing back, and a stream of compassion went through her. She reached out and grabbed his hand. "It might. But it's not something I would do. I'd never cheat on someone."

His fingers squeezed around hers, his gaze steady on hers for a moment. "No, I don't think you would. I'm sorry for even thinking it."

"I can see how it might have come across." And she understood why he had jumped to that conclusion. And she ached for him. What would it be like to have someone you trusted betray you so horribly? Parker may have been a lot of things, but at least he'd never cheated on her.

He let go of her hand. "So what you wanted to talk about, does it have something to do with why you were so upset at the park?"

And here they went. She'd thought and thought, but the right words just wouldn't come. "This would be so much easier if neither of us remembered the other from that night in Cozumel." She closed her eyes and whispered. "*So* much easier. For both of us."

The room seemed to shift for a second as he continued to process the fact that she hadn't cheated on him. When she'd first said that Avery was someone special to her, he'd been angry. Furious, even, that she would use him to cheat on her significant other. It had brought back the memory of finding out how Tanya had behaved with his best man.

Only it had somehow hit him so much harder thinking that Serena had cheated on someone with him, and he had no idea why.

And now she was acting like Cozumel had had so little impact that they might have forgotten the other existed?

He stared at her. Then one side of his mouth unexpectedly went up. "You think I could *ever* forget that night? Or you?"

"Oh." Her teeth came down on her lip. "I—I didn't quite mean—"

"I remember everything. Every. Little. Thing. Including a certain little butterfly." Right on cue, his body responded to the memory. When he'd seen her with that other guy at the luncheon, he'd been so sure they were lovers. The hand touch, the steady way they looked at each other. The kiss. The thought of that man kissing her tiny tattoo had made something in his stomach drop.

He'd decided then and there that the man had something to do with what she'd said at the park that day. With her teary request that he not ask her anything else about it.

The relief he felt in discovering they were just friends was way out of proportion to the situation. Why should it matter to him at all?

He leaned forward and cupped her cheek.

All common sense seemed to retreat to the back of his brain and cower in a corner as a sudden need began to thrum through him, and the blood coursing through his veins began to pick up speed.

Because dammit all. It was true. He remembered everything about that night, including the wild satisfaction of feeling her flesh close around his and grip tightly until he… He wanted that again. Wanted to lay her on his desk and make her feel what she'd made him feel that night.

Her lips parted, the tiniest bit.

Her hair was in wild disarray, like it was

on most days. But it was sexy. So, so sexy. Bedroom hair. And the feeling as he'd gathered all those luxurious silky locks together and…

"Toby…"

He wasn't sure if it was a question or a plea, but the shaky longing in her whisper swept through him like a typhoon, hurling away everything in its path. Their chairs were on wheels, and he yanked hers closer in a rush, his knees pushing between hers in a way that made his breath seize in his chest.

Her mouth was inches from his, and he hesitated a fraction of a second. Just long enough to make the first touch that much sweeter before giving in to his body's demands. His hands gripped the arms of her chair as hot coals licked at his innards, igniting an inferno of lust. The touch of her tongue at the corner of his mouth was his final undoing. His hands left the arms of the chair and slid around her hips to cup her butt. With a single hard movement, he hauled her onto his lap, relishing the tiny moan she gave as she came fully against him.

Yes.

He hid his face in her neck, the wild beat

of her pulse against his lips, making him want to throw caution to the wind, as if there'd been any other option.

This was the woman she'd been in Mexico: fueled by the evidence of his neediness. Desperate to touch and be touched.

His hands buried themselves in her heavy hair, his mouth going back to hers. His tongue didn't hesitate. It dove inside her mouth, that first plunge sending him to hell and back. He wanted her.

Needed her.

No matter what the cost.

As if sensing his thoughts, she eased her mouth from his and went up on her knees, and he gripped her hips to help her keep her balance. She slowly slid her white gauzy skirt up her thighs, her hair dancing around her face as she looked down at him.

He swallowed. "Damn, Serena. You are so beautiful."

"I could say the same about you." Biting her lip in that seductive way she had, she murmured. "Undo your zipper, and I'll let you see my butterfly." The slow swirl of her hips made him think the words had more than one meaning.

He pulled her forward and kissed her stomach, then said, "Give me a sec."

He barely had enough room to get his hand into his back pocket to get his wallet out and remove something from it. Then he undid his zipper and freed himself. One hand slid under her blouse and found her breast, squeezing and stroking. Her eyes fluttered shut. He lifted the condom packet he'd taken out to his mouth with his free hand and tore it open, somehow managing to roll it down himself.

With that done, he slid his hands up her back and carried her shirt over her head.

Lacy bra. Covering what he wanted to see. He undid it and let it fall free.

There.

His fingertips touched the wing of the tiny creature decorating her breast. Palming her back, he eased her forward until he could reach it. The tip of his tongue slowly traced over the tattoo, his arm going around her bottom and pressing her against his chest as his mouth shifted from the butterfly to her nipple. The first suck was so satisfying. So sexy. And those damned sounds she was making was going to make him come apart long before he was ready. His hands went to her hips and urged her to straddle him again, until all that was between them was her panties.

She rocked against him, making his world go multicolored as he used his tongue, his lips, his teeth to bring her as much pleasure as she was bringing him. Her arms went around his head, holding him to her breast. Not that he was planning on going anywhere.

But he wanted more. Wanted it all. Sliding the elastic on her remaining undergarment to the side, he pressed his fingers against her pubic bone as his thumb touched her most intimate area, before moving deeper, finding heat. Moist, sexy heat. He wanted to sink deep into her and lose himself in a rush. But he remembered exactly how satisfying it had been to hold himself on the brink. To force himself to wait. And wait. And wait.

The crazy intimacy of their position… He groaned. They were close. So close that touching her meant he was touching himself too.

And it was hotter than anything he'd ever done with a woman.

"Dios... Ahora, Tobias... Ahora."

His whispered name came out in accented Spanish, and instinctively he knew exactly what she meant. Taking himself in hand, he positioned himself, but she wasn't waiting. As soon as she felt him, she pushed down, hard, her hands gripping his shoulders, head thrown back.

He filled his hands with her curves, matching his rhythm to hers, driving up each time she came down.

"Tobias..."

Her movements grew more frantic, and with each movement she pushed him closer to a cliff. One that he wanted and yet didn't want to leap off.

Then she seated herself fully. "Ahh!"

He felt it. The desperate, squeezing pulse that did what he'd been trying to avoid. Holding her against him, he thrust and thrust until the ecstasy ripped everything from him, leaving him vulnerable and exposed. Yet he kept moving, each stroke a little slower, a little more replete. And then he was still, his breathing unsteady, brain in a whirl.

It took him a second to realize she was

leaning back looking at him and had said something.

And she was staring at him in a way that made tension gather in his loose muscles. A strange tension that said something was about to change forever.

Serena waited for him to say something. To respond to what she'd just told him. She was horrified that she'd sat here in his office and had sex with him instead of having the hard conversation she'd come here to have. But she never quite thought straight when she was around him. And to have blurted out that she was pregnant so soon after making love with him again... None of this was happening the way she'd wanted it to.

But now that she'd said it, she couldn't take the words back.

He blinked as if not quite sure what to say. "Sorry?" He shifted her on his legs, easing out of her.

She hated the feeling but understood that he was probably in shock. Maybe she should backtrack and try this again.

"I... I..." She took a deep breath. "I haven't

been feeling quite right for the last couple of weeks, and I couldn't figure out why."

"You didn't look like you felt at all well when we were running. And add that to what you said before we parted ways…"

Her teeth scraped against each other a couple of times as she tried to drum up the courage to say again what she needed to say. "I couldn't get up the nerve to tell you what was wrong that day."

"And now you want to."

He looked confused. Maybe Toby hadn't actually heard what she'd said a minute ago. She hadn't exactly shouted out the news. "Yes. As I said, I wasn't feeling well and realized my cycle was later than it had ever been. So… I decided to take a pregnancy test."

"I see."

He was calm. Too calm.

A sense of horror and foreboding rushed over her. "I'm pregnant. And as you now know, Avery is not the father. Although I'm sure you might wish he were."

"You're pregnant?"

The words were said with that same strange calmness even as her brain was still busy staggering back to its feet after what they'd just done together.

Why was he staring at her as if he still didn't understand what she was saying?

He repeated the words once again before he blinked. "Oh, hell. *I'm* the father?"

This time his voice wasn't monotone, and although he hadn't shouted it at her, his words nevertheless struck her with the force of a sledgehammer.

She scrambled off him. "I'm so sorry. I just thought you should know." She licked her lips as she stood there in complete disarray, the fact that she was naked from the waist up barely registering with her. "I should never have…" She motioned at the chair he still sat in.

Should never have what? Let him make love to her?

Yes. Exactly that. Except she'd been so caught up in his words as he said he could never forget that night, or her, that she couldn't think clearly. She'd been bewitched by him. Just like she had been at the bar in Cozumel. Only none of that was his fault. She never should have let him make love to her before he knew the truth about why she'd wanted to speak to him.

But there was no going back now.

Even though he'd made it more than clear before this that he didn't want to be a father. At least not at this point in his life.

And maybe not ever.

Toby stared at her as he tried to clear his head. He didn't want to be a father. Didn't want to be involved with anyone. Didn't feel he was capable of sustaining any kind of relationship, much less that of father and child. And yet, he'd just…

With quick jerky movements, she righted her panties and skirt and pulled on her bra and shirt. Parts of his body that had gone numb, twitched for a second before he got them back under control.

Dammit! Say something!

But there were no words he could think of to say. And as much as he wanted to wish this away, he couldn't. It was real.

Serena seemed to give up on him having any other response, because she ran her palms down her skirt. "Even though I felt you should know, please believe me when

I say that I don't expect anything from you. Don't want anything from you. I am fully prepared to—I *want* to do this on my own."

Her reasons for not liking to run alone came back to him vividly, and yet, he still had no idea what to say to her. He couldn't even believe this was happening. The words that finally came out of his mouth were insane. And totally insulting.

"I know you said you and Avery aren't together, but was there no one else? You're sure it's mine?"

She should have slapped him. Screamed at him. Called him all manner of names. But she didn't. She just stood there for a minute and stared at him.

Her question, when it came, was so quiet he almost missed it. "What do you think?"

Remorse clawed through his conscience until he couldn't stand it any longer. "I don't know why I said that. I have no excuse other than being caught off guard."

"Don't worry about it." She walked over to the door before looking back. "And we never have to talk about any of this again."

She motioned to the chairs. "Not about what happened in this room. Or what happened in Cozumel. Or what is going to happen from here on."

With that, she headed out of the room, closing the door behind her.

Was the pain of that last encounter ever going to fade? She was on day three since their encounter in his office, and it was still there. Still churning in her stomach every time she thought about what had happened.

She'd toyed with the idea of resigning and trying to find a nursing position somewhere else, but how would she explain to a prospective employer that she'd quit less than a month after being hired? It didn't look very good. And by the time she found something else, she'd be even further along in her pregnancy.

Paz Memorial was her dream job. But right now, she couldn't imagine working with Toby day in and day out. She loved working the trauma cases, loved watching Toby's expertise and skill. But in her head, she could still hear the shock in his voice as he asked her if she was sure the baby was his. It hadn't been a question, exactly. And yet, it was obvious a sliver of doubt was there.

Because he didn't want it to be his.

That's what it boiled down to. She hadn't expected him to be overcome with happiness and start picking out baby names. But even without meaning to, he'd wounded her deeply with his words, and she wasn't sure she could get over it.

Maybe the best course of action would be to wait until the baby was born, then give her notice and start looking for another job. But that was something she could do after having some more time to think. Because today, she just felt tired and sad and out of sorts.

But she would get through it.

To his credit, Toby didn't ask what she was going to do, although he'd probably realized by her coming to him that she was going to keep the baby. Talking about how she was going to do it on her own had made it pretty clear. And if she'd been going to have an abortion, she wouldn't have even told him about the pregnancy.

Toby hadn't shown up for work yesterday or today. The thought that maybe he was going to be the one to quit zipped through her system. That was probably part of her sadness. She didn't want that either. He belonged here. It was clear he was well loved and highly respected.

She'd finished working out her shift after they'd had sex and then had gone home and cried on Avery's shoulder. She couldn't even remember what he'd said to her, but she'd finally stumbled to her feet and fallen into bed. The next morning, she'd been a little more clearheaded and thought she might go back and reassure Toby yet again that he didn't have anything to worry about. That she knew he didn't want children and had no intention of trying to saddle him with one.

But how could she explain the sex to him when she couldn't even explain it to herself? When he'd reached for her in his office, she'd been so relieved that he wanted her that she'd let her emotions take over. Maybe part of her obliviousness had been born out of some dreamland that wanted everyone to live happily ever after.

Well, her mom hadn't gotten that kind of ending, so why would she expect to? Yet she wouldn't be really going it completely on her own, no matter what happened. She had her mom and some good friends, including Avery. She would need their love and support now more than ever. They would be the safety net she had when things got tough. In fact, when she'd called her mom and told her about the baby, her mom had been both thrilled and sympathetic. "I could relocate to San Diego if you want, Serena. I can write anywhere."

She'd reassured her mom that she would call on her if she needed her but that there was no need to move. If anyone would be relocating, it would be Serena. But that was a decision she could make further down the line. Who knew? She might even miscarry, although even the thought had her laying a protective hand over her belly.

It might solve a whole lot of problems, but she definitely did not want to lose this baby. Instead, she found herself already imagining what the baby would look like. How it would feel to hold them in her arms...

She finished checking on her patients and then headed back to the nurses' station to catch up on some paperwork while she could.

Shuffling through a couple of computer screens to find the one she wanted, she glanced up when she heard the elevator ping. The doors opened and Toby got off. He looked at her, and at first, she thought he was going to walk right past her without saying anything, but then he moved toward the desk.

"When you get a chance, could I have a quick word?"

She gulped back a queasy sensation of panic.

"Um, yes. As soon as Jacelyn comes back from break. Do you want me to come by your office?"

His jaw went tight for a minute before he shook his head. "Can you text me when you're free and meet me down in the court-yard?"

Did he think she was going to jump him in his office…again?

No, of course he didn't. She was being ri-diculous. And she shouldn't want to meet him in a private place either, after what had happened last time. Although from the look on his face, the last thing he wanted from her was sex.

"Yes, I will."

"Thanks."

Lord, he had this defeated look on his face that made her cringe. It brought the hurt roar-

ing back to life. Or maybe she was project-
ing her own feelings onto him.

Except she suddenly didn't feel defeated.
She was having a baby. One that was going
to be loved and wanted, if only by her and a
handful of her family and friends. But that
was enough.

She'd done the right thing in telling Toby
and had tried her best to reassure him that
she didn't want anything from him. She
couldn't help it that he didn't want the baby.

Of course, she hadn't wanted a positive
pregnancy test either. At first. But now?

Yes, she was happy. Not about the way that
it had happened, but that the decision about
the "right time" had been taken out of her
hands. Because left to her own devices, she
might never have taken the leap on her own.

Jacelyn came back a half hour later and
told her to go ahead and take off. Serena
had made an appointment with the OB-
GYN she'd met the day of Lucinda's arm
gash, Gary Rollings. She'd really liked him.
She'd thought about going to an outside hospital to have more privacy, but really, what
was the point? It was going to become obvious pretty quickly that she was pregnant.

She already had an answer ready for anyone who might ask about the father: he wasn't in the picture.

Because it was true. And actually, that was okay. To try and force a relationship for the sake of a baby usually only ended in disaster. And the last thing she wanted was for Toby to try to "do the right thing by her." Because it wasn't the right thing. For either of them.

So why had she had sex with him again with such eagerness?

She had a ready answer for that too: he was good at it. And maybe it had felt like they had unfinished business from Cozumel. Well, that business was good and done now.

She smiled. He'd made it sound like she was unforgettable. That was probably at the crux of why she'd fallen back into his arms.

She typed a message on her phone.

On my way to the courtyard.

A second later, he texted that he would be down in a minute.

Once she got there, all she could do was wait.

CHAPTER SEVEN

Toby had needed a couple of days to think about things. And it had boiled down to some pretty basic facts.

Fact one: he didn't want to be a father.

Fact two: he was going to be a father whether he wanted to be one or not.

Fact three: none of this was Serena's or the baby's fault.

Fact four: he was not going to make Serena do this on her own.

That last one was the key and the one he wanted to talk about. None of the rest of it mattered. What mattered was what he was going to do from here. If she would even hear him out.

If she refused… Well, he couldn't force her to accept his help, but he did want to offer it up in a way that was sincere and honest.

So he hoped to hell he didn't make as big a mess out of this as he had the last time they'd talked.

It was part of the reason he wanted the meeting to happen in a public place. The woman did something to his head and reached into places he'd thought he'd closed and locked. Well, he'd now reinforced those locks and had learned some valuable lessons in the process.

Getting off the elevator, he grabbed a coffee from the cafeteria, taking a chance and getting a decaf for her, picking up all kinds of packets and flavorings and hoping that she'd like something in the bag of stuff.

When he pushed through the doors and entered the San Diego heat, he spotted her immediately. And in front of her was a paper coffee cup.

That made him smile. Maybe he hadn't been as far off as he'd thought.

He made his way over to her and sat down on the curved bench in front of her, a sense of déjà vu coming over him. How long ago had they sat here and eaten lunch? Not all that long, but right now it seemed like forever ago.

"Hi. I brought you something, but I see you've already got some coffee."

"How did you know how I like it?"

His smiled widened. "Well…" He dumped out his bag of offerings.

"Oh, my." Her brows went up. "I don't put *quite* that much stuff in it."

"Let me hazard a guess." He separated out sugar packets and vanilla creamer and slid them toward her. "Right?"

"Wrong." She pushed the items back into the pile, and her fingers swirled around the choices for a few seconds before she shrugged and brought her hand back to her coffee, fingers curling around the cup.

"I didn't see any other—"

"That's because there isn't anything else to put in it. Because I like it black."

That shouldn't have surprised him, but it did. Hell, did he stereotype yoga practitioners? That stuff had been pretty damned difficult to do. A lot harder than plunking one foot in front of the other for an hour, like he did with running.

He held his hands up palms out. "Okay, you got me. Caffeinated or decaf?"

"Normally I like full test, but things have

changed on my end. I still like the taste, though."

"At least I got that part right." Leaning forward, he looked at her. "I want you to know that I realize I handled things poorly the other day."

"No, you didn't. I'm pretty sure this was an outcome neither of us expected. Both in Cozumel and in your office. I meant it when I said I don't expect anything from you. And while I in no way planned to get pregnant, I can't bring myself to regret it." There was a moment of hesitation before she continued. "I should have come out with it right when we got to your office. Before things got out of hand."

"I don't think either one of us expected what happened in that office." His smile was a little weaker as he weighed his next words. "I'm here to ask how I can help."

"Help?"

"I want to be there for you. For the baby. We can take turns with parenting duties and—"

"Absolutely not."

Shock held him silent for a second. "I'm sorry?"

"You made it pretty clear how you felt about having kids the last time we were in this courtyard. And your reaction in your office only reaffirmed my suspicions." She shrugged. "My telling you had nothing to do with expecting you to take on any parenting duties. I just didn't feel right about keeping it a secret from you. Someday, they might want to know who their father is. Better for you to be shocked now than to be shocked then."

He frowned. "And you think it's okay to tell that child about a parent who played no role in their upbringing, who thinks he didn't…want…them?"

"Well, you don't, so—"

"You're right, Serena. I didn't want or expect to have a child. Not right now, anyway, if ever. But I am having one." He paused to suck down a breath. "The same way you didn't expect to have a baby, but you are *choosing* to have this child rather than terminating the pregnancy. In the same way that I am *choosing*—for lack of a better term—to have a role in the child's life. It's not out of duty or obligation. I want to be there."

She didn't say anything for a long, long moment. "What if you change your mind?"

"I won't. You'll find I'm a pretty black-and-white kind of guy. I don't want to be in a relationship. I can't offer you that. But I would like to be a father to this child."

"I never expected us to be in a relationship. I don't want that either. My mom and dad didn't have a good marriage, and I'd honestly rather be on my own than risk getting involved for the wrong reasons. Or with the wrong person."

"I agree with you. I've been there too, and it wasn't the greatest experience." He gave a pained laugh. "Cozumel was supposed to be my honeymoon, actually."

"I'd heard. I'm so sorry."

His mouth cocked to the side. "I should have figured someone would tell you. Anyway, I went there for the purpose of committing my life to my job and nothing else."

"And then you met me." Her eyes went big, and she stuttered for a second before saying, "I'm talking about the pregnancy, not about us being involved romantically."

"I got it."

"I never did get a chance to thank you for stepping in between me and that guy in the bar."

"No thanks were needed." He smiled at her. "So can we try to figure out how this is going to work?"

"Yes… But I'd really rather no one at the hospital know who the father is right away. If I miscarry, it could make it even more awkward than it's eventually going to be."

He frowned. "Have you been having any symptoms that might suggest a miscarriage?"

"No. I didn't mean that. Just that some pregnancies don't make it for one reason or another. There are no guarantees."

The thought of her losing the baby bothered him on a level that surprised him. "Have you seen a doctor yet?"

"No, but I've made an appointment with Gary Rollings. It's a couple of weeks away."

"Gary's a pretty discreet guy. I'd like to come with you to that appointment. But I'll understand if you'd rather I didn't."

Serena looked surprised. "Can I think about it?"

"Of course. Take all the time you need." He couldn't blame her. It was one thing to let him be a part of their child's life. But he understood that she needed to mark out some boundary lines and stick to them.

"I do have a question. I wasn't going to ask, but since you're here…" She shook her head. "Is there any genetic stuff from your side of the family that I should know about?"

That hadn't dawned on him. But then again, neither had a lot of things. "I had an aunt with early-onset breast cancer, but it's the only thing I can think of right now."

"Okay, thanks."

"Anything else?" He wanted to know if she had any other reservations or questions. He was a little worried that this meeting had gone better than he'd expected it to. Was halfway expecting the bottom to drop out at any moment.

"Just one thing."

He tensed. And here it came. "Okay."

"I would like to pick the baby's name."

It was so far from what he'd expected her to say that it made him laugh. The tension drained from his body. "Well as long as you don't choose something like Fig or Tree, I don't think we have a problem."

She smiled back at him. "I think I can work within those parameters."

The next three days seemed to go pretty well. Even though she hadn't asked the question she'd really wanted to ask him out on that terrace. She'd actually chickened out and blurted the wanting-to-pick-the-name thing when what she'd really wanted to ask was whether or not he felt like they could continue working together under the circumstances.

But he'd given no indication that he couldn't. She'd shared an operating room with him twice since he'd been back, and he'd been courteous and respectful, if a little bit stiff.

She couldn't blame him. They'd had sex in his office, for heaven's sake, and they were having a child together. Yet looking at it through objective eyes, they really didn't know each other all that well.

But then, had she really known Parker either? Oh, she'd thought she had, but it turned out she had had a romanticized view of him that hadn't held up to scrutiny. He'd probably felt the same way about her.

She also needed to decide whether she wanted Toby there for her appointments or not. Her gut feeling was to hold that part of herself aside. Letting him be there...

It felt possibly a little too intimate, despite the fact that they'd had sex twice. Sex, though, was different from intimacy, as she'd learned from her relationship with Parker.

Plus, it would be much easier to keep her secret if no one, not even the OB-GYN, knew the truth other than her and Toby. Well, aside from Avery.

She hadn't actually told Toby that Avery knew either. But he did know that they were close friends, so surely he would figure it out.

Right now, though, she couldn't worry about any of that. She needed to concentrate on staying well and healthy. So far, her morning sickness had been fairly mild. Just that occasional queasiness that left as quickly as it came. It was one of the reasons she hadn't realized she was pregnant until she'd started counting the days.

Her phone buzzed on her hip. Glancing at the screen, she frowned. It was Toby.

Uh-oh.

"Hello?"

"Hey, are you still on duty?"

She hesitated. "Yes, but I'm getting ready to leave. Is there an emergency?"

"No emergency. I was just headed for the beach and thought you might like to join me."

She was surprised by the invitation, actually, and an alarm went off inside of her. Maybe he'd changed his mind about the whole thing. "Any particular reason?"

"Friday is just normally my beach day. I like to sit and listen to the surf. It's something I thought I might like to do with the baby. I'll understand if you'd rather not come, though."

"Actually, that sounds pretty good. It's been a rough day."

There was a pause. "Everything okay?"

She mentally filled in the blanks, since the word *miscarriage* had previously been mentioned. She was actually touched that he sounded a little concerned. "Yep, it was just a busy day."

"Got it. Meet you at the door to the parking garage?"

"No bathing suits needed, right?"

"Are you suggesting what I think you're suggesting?"

The obviousness of his comment made her laugh for what felt like the first time since their talk in the courtyard. "I'm not suggesting anything of the sort. Give me about fifteen minutes, okay?"

"You got it."

She disconnected, feeling a relief that bordered on giddiness. Maybe this would all work out after all.

Twenty minutes later, they were in Toby's SUV, navigating the streets of San Diego. "You really go to the beach every Friday?"

He nodded. "I think it's my yoga."

"Not quite the same thing, but I get it. It's how you recharge."

"Exactly."

She halfway expected him to press her for answers about going to the doctor together, but he didn't. Instead, they talked about cases. Some that they'd worked together and some separate. It almost felt like what she and Avery did on occasion. Except this man definitely wasn't Avery.

Whereas she felt she could be totally herself with her roommate, she didn't have that same easy relationship with Toby. And maybe that was because of Cozumel. What she'd thought had been a fun, no-strings-attached romp in a hotel room had turned into something more complicated than anything she could imagine.

It was confusing. And scary in a way she didn't understand.

She'd talked to her mom about it, although she hadn't given any names. But her mom's only advice had been to follow her heart. Then again, her mom had done that too, and it hadn't exactly ended well. But her mom was wiser now. She hadn't jumped back into a relationship, and it had been five years since Serena's dad had died.

Maybe she no longer trusted her instincts.

Kind of like Serena? While Parker hadn't scarred her for life, it had made her wary of what lay just beneath the surface in any man that might have caught her interest.

Including Toby. He'd been a study in contradictions in some ways. And yet, he seemed to be as steady as a rock when it came to his job. But, like her, he already had one failed relationship in his past.

She blew out a silent breath. She just couldn't think about this right now.

"Almost there."

Maybe her sigh hadn't been as quiet as

she'd thought. "It's fine. I'm still not sure why you invited me to come."

"I thought it might be good if we got to know each other a little better, since we'll be seeing quite a bit of each other outside of work."

She wasn't sure that completely answered her question, but she could hazard a guess. "Because of the baby."

"Yes. And I'd like you to know what kind of man I am outside of work."

Okay, so this was more about reassuring her that he was no serial killer? She had to remember that he had no interest in her personally. That circumstances had dragged them together, and he was trying to make the best of things. So the least she could do was try to meet him halfway and do the same.

She glanced at him. "So tell me something I don't know about you."

"Hmm… I, um, have a cat."

"Seriously?"

"Seriously, although I kind of inherited her."

Before she could think of a response to that, he tossed the same question back at her.

She grinned at him. "I like country music. And line dancing."

His brows went up. "I find that more surprising than the yoga."

A laugh squeaked out before she could stop it. "Are you saying you're not a fan?"

"Not saying that. I like all kinds of music." He pulled into one of the area parking lots and found a spot.

Nice. She couldn't have picked a better place.

"I love Mission Beach." It was one of the larger beaches in the area, with a long stretch of sand. Since he'd said he liked to come and sit near the ocean, she figured he wasn't into the rich nightlife that the area also offered. She wasn't either. So it made it even funnier that both of them had wound up in a strobe-lit bar in Mexico.

"It's my favorite spot."

They made their way past the boardwalk and onto the beach. It was still pretty early, but some of the sun worshippers were starting to gather their things, so it wasn't hard to find a spot on the sand.

They didn't have towels, but it was okay. There was something warm and grounding about sitting on actual sand. "I don't get to come out here very much anymore," she murmured, half to herself.

"I finally had to decide I was going to make an effort to drive out here. Otherwise, things get crowded out by all the noise of life."

She could understand that. She'd done that very thing, which was why when she'd realized she was pregnant, she'd had to look at her life and decide what was really important. Mabel's words had come back to her, and she realized she could do this. She could be a mom. And that now was as good a time as any.

"So what's your cat's name?"

"Porkchop."

She stared at him, trying to decide if he was telling the truth.

He smiled. "It really is. It was the name she came with."

"Came with? From where? A pig farm?"

His chuckle washed over her like one of the waves that lapped against the shore. She found that she liked the sound of it.

"No, she came from a shelter. I think maybe it was partly a joke. She has a tan spot on her side that kind of looks like a, well, a pork chop."

"Too funny."

They sat there for a few minutes without speaking, and as the sounds of the surf continued to rumble, Serena could feel her muscles unwinding. Maybe this really was like yoga, only without the physical effort. She flopped back onto the sand and closed her eyes for a few minutes, just listening. Absorbing what was around her. There was music and human interaction. The squawking of gulls as they flew overhead. The ocean as it pushed forward and then retreated.

She opened her eyes and turned to her head to find Toby watching her.

"What?"

He didn't say anything for a minute, just reached over and brushed a strand of hair from her forehead. The act made her shiver.

Then he said, "Thanks for telling me."

She knew what he was talking about. And those simple words pulled at something deep inside of her, threatening to call up feelings that she'd rather stayed buried deep. Threatened to forge new brain pathways that she definitely couldn't cope with right now.

Rather than examine any of that, she just looked back at him and said, "You're welcome."

A sharp cry came from the boardwalk area behind them.

Serena sat up in a rush to find that Toby was already on his feet. "Where's it coming from?"

The scream came again.

"Up there." They ran to the boardwalk access and found an elderly man lying on the asphalt surface with people already gathering around him.

"Call 911." Toby pushed through, telling people he was a doctor, while Serena dialed emergency services.

By the time she joined him, he was already examining an area on the gentleman's head that was bleeding profusely. He glanced at her. "He tried to step out of the way of someone on rollerblades and lost his balance. He hit his head on the concrete wall."

She winced as she looked at the thick concrete that separated the boardwalk from the beach.

He had his phone out and turned on the

flashlight setting as he peered into the man's eyes. He swore softly.

"One of his pupils is blown." He looked around the crowd. "Does anyone know him?"

There were head shakes indicating those nearby didn't know who he was, and no one stepped forward with any information until someone finally said, "I think he's homeless. I've seen him walking down here before."

Serena's heart ached, as she heard the faint sound of a siren in the distance.

Careful not to move him, Toby patted the man's pockets, probably hoping to find some ID, but he looked at her and shook his head. She moved next to him and monitored his pulse while Toby went to flag down the paramedics. They were there in minutes, bringing a gurney while Toby explained that he thought the man had a skull fracture.

Together, they put a neck brace on him, carefully slid a backboard underneath him and loaded him into the back of the vehicle.

It all happened so fast that Serena wasn't even sure it actually *had* happened. One minute they were on the beach and the next they were in emergency mode. "Do you want to follow them in?"

"No. They've already called the hospital and will have a trauma team waiting for him. We'll be five steps behind."

She shivered, wrapping her arms around herself. "I hate that he was all alone." He'd looked so small lying there. So frail.

"So do I." He glanced at her. "No one should ever have to feel that way."

Was he still talking about the injured man? Or about their own situation. Serena was suddenly bone-weary. So much had happened over the last several weeks. So many changes to her life that it was overwhelming.

"Do you mind if we go back to the hospital?"

"Are you okay?"

"Yeah. I think so. Just tired. I think I'm going to get in my car and call it a night."

Not that night had even officially darkened the sky. But right now, she felt like she could sleep for a week. There'd been something so vulnerable looking in Toby's face as he'd leaned over her, thanking her for telling him about the pregnancy.

She'd never quite seen that in him before, and she wasn't sure how to deal with it. Because somehow, he'd succeeded in tunneling into her heart when she wasn't paying attention and was now taking up residence there.

She needed to do one of two things: Either send him an eviction notice and kick him out. Or somehow learn to make peace with his presence.

CHAPTER EIGHT

HE HADN'T EXPECTED the man from the boardwalk to make it, but when Toby arrived at work the next morning and asked at the nurse's desk, he'd been told the man was in ICU but very much alive.

He decided to head over there and check on him, since his floor was quiet at the moment.

The second he stepped through the doors, he was struck by the difference between the surgical area and these rooms. Surgery could be loud or not so loud, but there was always a lot of movement, with staff leaning over beds and fighting to save lives.

ICU was quiet. So quiet, it was eerie. This was also a place where the fight to save lives happened, but it was a completely different type of fight.

He went to the desk and was told they were calling him Patient Doe for the moment. So far, no one was looking for him. At least not that they knew of. And he'd had no ID at all on him. The nurse nodded at the room number. "He's a popular guy today."

Toby frowned but went into the room.

Serena sat on a chair beside the bed. He shouldn't have been overly surprised that she'd beaten him to the punch. "I should have known."

She turned around and looked at him. "I had to check. They said no one has come forward yet."

"I'm sure they're checking some of the local services to see if anyone knows him. But at least he's still fighting. And social services will be called in to assess him if he really is alone."

"Are you working today?"

"Yep. You?"

"I'm actually off." She glanced at him. "Oh, and if you want to go with me to my first OB-GYN appointment, you can. If you're free, that is."

What had made her change her mind? He'd been almost positive she'd been going to tell him no. "Text me the day and time when you get a chance, and I'll put in on my calendar."

Even if he had to move things around, he was going to do his damnedest to be there.

"Okay, I will. Will you let me know if there's any change in his condition?"

Serena had come in on her day off just to check on their John Doe. She could have called, but instead, she'd come in person. Something shifted inside of him without warning and got lodged somewhere in his chest. "I will. Hopefully he'll pull through."

"Yes. Hopefully." She glanced up at him. "How's Porkchop?"

"She's fine."

She smiled. "I halfway thought you were pulling my leg yesterday."

"Nope, I wasn't." He pulled his phone out and scrolled through some pictures until he got to an image of his cat. He turned it around so she could see.

"Oh, my gosh. She really does have a marking. And it looks exactly like a pork chop."

"Told you."

"Well, on that note, I think I'll head home. I'll text you that date."

He nodded. "Appreciate it."

As he watched her walk away, hips swaying slightly under the same gauzy skirt she'd worn that day in his office, he glanced at the picture of the cat—his only current commitment—and hoped to hell he was doing the right thing in agreeing to take on a child.

These were real lives. Lives that could be hurt. Or disappointed. He'd already disappointed one woman. He sure as hell didn't want to be responsible for disappointing another one, because this one came with consequences that were a lot weightier than falling in or out of love.

This was a child's future. And somehow, he was going to have figure out how to balance it gingerly in his hands and keep on doing it for the next eighteen years and beyond.

Almost as soon as he digested that fact, his phone pinged, and he glanced down at it. It was a notation with the time and date of Serena's appointment with Gary Rollings at his private practice. Counting down the numbers in his head, he realized it was only a week and a half away. Even as he thought it, an internal clock began some kind of countdown, clicking off seconds and pushing them behind him. Forever. One after the other.

This was real. Far too real. He lowered himself into the chair and stared at John Doe's silent form for several seconds, wondering exactly how he was going to father a child when he had no idea how to do that.

Serena came in to work the next day and stopped at the desk on the surgical floor to see if there was anything critical that needed her attention. It was still quiet. She was a few minutes early, so she was going down to check on the elderly man they'd helped on the boardwalk. Just as she started to turn back toward the elevators, Toby appeared from the hallway where his office was.

"Hey, I was just getting ready to go down to see if—"

She stopped when he shook his head, the look on his face making her blink. "What?"

"He didn't make it."

"What? What happened?"

He took a step closer. "He had a massive brain bleed."

"But he was stable when I left."

"I know. I was still in the room with him when he coded."

"You mean last night? How long were you there?"

"Just a little while. There was nothing that could be done."

A little white speck of energy slid up her spine and lodged in her neck. "You said you'd let me know if there was any change."

"I know I did. But there was nothing you could do. And you were probably still on your way home."

The energy expanded and circled a nerve center, setting it off. "I wouldn't have asked you to contact me if I didn't want to know." She worked to keep those words low and even.

His head tilted, probably not sure why she was so upset.

In truth, she wasn't sure why she was either. Was it about the man's passing? Or about Toby's circumventing her wishes?

"I understand that. Which is why I waited for you to come in this morning to tell you in person. I didn't want the news to come from a text or a phone call."

Her anger fizzled away in a rush. Okay,

so she'd guessed wrong about his motivation. "Sorry."

He waited as if expecting some further explanation. But what could she say? *I thought you were acting like my father*?

He hadn't been. But she'd expected him to on some level. Maybe because Parker had displayed some of those same characteristics once they'd moved in together. But it didn't mean that Toby was the same kind of person.

She turned around and leaned a hip against the nurse's desk, which was empty at the moment. They were probably doing last-minute checks before the shift change. "I really wanted him to make it."

"I know. So did I." He glanced at her clothes. "No yoga today?"

She couldn't prevent a smile from forming, despite the lump of sadness in her throat. "Already went. I just changed into work clothes before coming up. No running?"

"Same."

"Looks like we're creatures of habit."

She wasn't sure that was a good thing.

He joined her at the desk, crossing his arms over his chest. "Looks that way."

"Did they ever find out his identity?"

"No. They didn't."

Somehow, that was even sadder than his passing. It was like he'd slid from the world and disappeared without leaving a trace.

She touched her stomach. Was that part of what having kids was about? It wasn't just loving them and raising them. Maybe it was about making sure there was someone who kept the previous generation's memories alive.

Shaking off the morbid thought, she glanced at him. "So what's on the docket today?"

"Our liver laceration patient is being released this afternoon, so that's good news."

"Any more word on Mabel Tucker?"

He nodded. "She has an appointment tomorrow for a routine follow-up. She was supposed to get a couple of immunizations this past week. And her medical alert bracelet should arrive next week."

It was hard to believe she was the first patient they'd seen together. It seemed like ages ago. Maybe because so much had happened since then.

"All good news."

His blue eyes caught hers, and her tummy

shivered the way it always did when he looked at her.

Someone called her name, and she turned away from Toby in time to see her mom get off the elevator and start walking toward them. Oh, God. That was all she needed.

Her mom knew about the pregnancy, but Serena hadn't told her specifically about Toby yet, and she wasn't sure why. Hurrying over, she rattled off a string of Spanish asking when she'd arrived. And why.

Her mom glanced at Toby and then answered her in English. "Since when do I need a reason to visit my only daughter?"

Leave it to her mom to lay on the guilt. "You don't, of course. I just could have left a key to the apartment for you."

"I actually was in the area on the way to research a nearby town and thought I'd drop in." She glanced at Toby again. "Aren't you going to introduce me?"

"Oh, of course." She headed toward the desk, her mom close behind. "Toby Renfro, this is my mom, Gracia Dias." It was virtually impossible to say her mom's name without pronouncing it in Spanish. "Toby is a trauma surgeon here at the hospital."

Her mom gave her a long, searching look. "Is he now?"

Toby, evidently unaware of the unspoken messages being sent back and forth between mother and daughter, held out his hand. "I actually do work here at the hospital. Serena told me you're a writer?"

Oh, no. He was just going to add fuel to her mom's speculation.

Serena quickly added, "I've told a lot of people that."

Toby frowned, and she couldn't blame him. She was being ridiculous. Why was she avoiding telling her mom who he was?

Because she didn't want to get hurt.

More than that, she didn't want to give her mom any reason to hope that she and Toby might get together romantically. Because they weren't going to. She'd eventually explain it to her, but not here. Not at the hospital.

"I'm just starting my shift, Mom, so I'm sorry I can't take you back to the apartment." She pulled her keys from her pocket and took the one to her apartment off the ring. "I'm not sure if Avery will be there or not when you get there, so just ring the bell rather than go right in." She didn't think he'd be walking around in the nude or anything, but since he thought she was at work…

"Well, I'll make you dinner, then. What time do you get off?"

"Five."

"And what time do you get off?" She fixed Toby with look. Serena could swear her mom had already guessed. How? They hadn't made googly eyes at each other, or even been standing that close together. But she had been thinking about how his blue eyes did it for her. Right as her mom got off the elevator.

"Mom, Toby doesn't want to eat with us."

"Actually, I wouldn't mind." His slow smile would have melted butter. "That is, if it's okay with you, Serena."

Oh, he was going to pay for that.

"Perfect. Then, it's settled. Dinner will be at seven, but come over whenever you get off work." Her mom didn't bother waiting for Serena to answer Toby's question about whether or not it was okay.

Was this the same woman who'd let herself get pushed around when Serena and Sergio were kids? She'd definitely come into her own. Serena couldn't be mad at her for that. And she wasn't. She was proud of her mom.

So very, very proud. And if that meant she cooked a meal for Toby and interrogated Serena without end, so be it. Serena wouldn't have it any other way.

She finally put her mom back in the elevator and told her to call when she got to the apartment, just as Jacelyn rounded the corner with a smile. "You got here early, Serena."

Yes, she had, and she was already exhausted from that scene with her mother. But since the other nurse was here, she couldn't grumble at Toby for letting himself get roped into dinner with them. If she knew her mom, it would be complete with candles and all the works.

"Well, I guess I'm going to go on rounds and check on a few patients." He gave her a wicked smile. "See you later."

Jacelyn waved at him while Serena sent him a glare, although she wasn't really mad. Just exasperated. The last thing she wanted to deal with today was having her mom and Toby in the same room.

But it looked like that was exactly what she was going to get, whether she wanted it or not.

Toby arrived at the house to find Serena's roommate heading out the door. "Dr. Renfro?"

"Yes. And you must be Avery."

"I am. Go on in. I'm actually headed to the hospital. But enjoy your dinner. It smells pretty great."

"Thanks."

Whether the other man knew about him or not was up in the air. But he was beginning to regret his impulse to tease Serena by allowing himself to be invited to dinner. She obviously hadn't told her mom about him. But he assumed she knew about the pregnancy. And if he had to guess, that was what had brought Gracia Dias to San Diego—not research. She probably wanted to see for herself that her daughter was okay. Who could blame her for that? It was so not like his parents, though. They'd given their son almost complete autonomy by the time he'd reached his teenage years. Curfews were never voiced, and Toby never once remembered his parents peeking in his room to make sure he was there.

He could see that was not how Serena was raised, and it made him tense. Was he sure he could do this? And he didn't just mean dinner.

He went through the open door in time to hear Serena talking to her mom in heated tones. The conversation was in Spanish, but he heard Gracia say his name a couple of times. Yep. This had definitely been a mistake.

He entered the room, making his presence known sooner rather than later by clearing his throat.

Serena saw him first, and her eyes widened. *"Mamá!"*

Her mom didn't look the slightest bit embarrassed. She just came over and stood on tiptoe, kissing him on the cheek.

"It's a custom." The words came from Serena, but she didn't need to explain.

"It's fine." He smiled at her mom, feeling warmed by the gesture, despite the fact that it was probably nothing more than a formality. "Nice to see you again. Thanks so much for inviting me."

"You're very welcome." She sent Serena a knowing smile.

Avery was right. The apartment smelled amazing. And the table was set with care. Long red tapers perched in the middle of it, along with a fresh bouquet of flowers. It was a mixture of daisies and roses.

"Go sit with Serena, while I finish a few things."

Serena sent him a look as she led him over to a couch, before mouthing *Sorry*.

"It's fine." He looked at her carefully. "Does she know about me?"

"Yep. And I didn't even tell her. But to deny it would have meant lying, and I couldn't bring myself to do that. She already knew about the pregnancy. Just not the rest."

"And Avery?"

"He knows too. I'm sorry. Here I am saying I want to keep it quiet, and I'm the one who's letting the cat out of the bag."

"If you trust Avery, then I do too. And your mom doesn't travel in the same circles as we do." He frowned as a thought came to him. "Were you going to tell her about me at all?"

She glanced away, telling him all he needed to know.

"So you weren't."

"Not right away. My mom, she's just…" She gave a small laugh. "A hopeless romantic."

"So the candles and the flowers…"

"Not meant to woo you, I promise. Not yet, anyway. She just likes to set a beautiful table. And daisies are my favorite flower, so she almost always gets some when she knows I'll be home."

"I didn't know they were your favorite flower."

She shrugged. "It's not something I go around telling everyone."

He tucked that piece of information away, not sure why, other than he didn't know a whole lot about her favorite things. He knew that she liked Mission Beach. And yoga. And that she drank her coffee black. And that she could mourn the death of someone she didn't even know.

Actually, there was a lot to like about Serena Dias.

"I think we are ready." Gracia came back into the room.

Toby got up and went over to the table with Serena, waiting for her to tell him where to sit. She must have noticed because she motioned to the chairs. "It doesn't matter. Avery and I rarely have time to eat together, so there aren't any assigned seats."

He opted for one of the plates in the middle of the table. Since there were four places, Gracia had evidently expected Avery to stay. "I passed your roommate in the hallway."

"Yes, he had to work. My mom's saving him enough food for tomorrow and probably several more days."

Her conspiratorial tones made him smile.

Gracia remained standing and served their plates. Serena was right. It was a huge meal, and he had no idea how she'd accomplished so much in so little time. There were enchiladas, beans and rice, guacamole with salad greens and tomatoes and a couple of side dishes he didn't recognize.

Serena gave a low groan. "I don't think I'll be doing yoga tomorrow after this meal."

"There's always running."

She made a face at him.

He liked this side of Serena. It was playful and just a tiny bit snarky. And it fit her to a tee. Strangely enough, despite her mom's vivid personality, Toby felt more relaxed than he'd felt in a long time. Maybe a little too relaxed.

As they ate, Gracia asked him about his work and what he liked about it and what he didn't.

"I was very proud of Serena for following her dream. I used to want to be a nurse. But…" She shrugged in a way that made him glance to his right at her daughter.

"But you followed another dream, *Mamá*."

"Yes, and I love it."

There was a brief lull in the conversation while they ate, before Gracia glanced at Serena. "Are you choosing baby names yet?"

"It's still too early. We'll, er, I'll do that later."

"Too early? Never. I had your name picked out before you were even conceived. I always knew your name would be Serena. It means *serene*. It fits her, no?"

He was pretty sure Serena was not feeling like her name right now. If anything, she looked flustered and maybe a little dismayed.

His own parents would never have made a dinner and invited his friends to join them.

It wasn't that they didn't care. His physical needs had always been met. But now that he was grown, he realized not all needs were physical. Some of his emotional needs had fallen by the wayside. It had instilled a fierce independence in him. To rely on someone else to meet his needs was a foreign concept to him. And the opposite was true as well. It made it hard for him to meet someone else's emotional needs. Because he wasn't always sure what they were. What he did know was that he didn't want his child to grow up thinking he didn't care about them. What kind of parent would he end up being? Warm and gracious and a bit of a bulldozer like Gracia? Or cool and reserved and completely hands-off like his own parents had been?

Shouldn't he be thinking about things like that? Whether or not he'd let his child pick out their own clothes. Or whether or not he'd make them eat their vegetables.

Like Serena said. It was still early. But in his head, he could still hear that *tick, tick, tick* of the seconds passing by.

She hasn't even had her first doctor's appointment yet.

So yes. Still very early days.

"Where do your parents live, Toby?"

"They're actually in Lancaster, where I'm from originally."

She offered him more food, but he shook his head. "I'm completely full, but thank you."

"You saved room for flan, I hope."

For some reason, he didn't think there was a choice involved. Serena gave him a quick shrug.

A minute later, Gracia was back with a picture-perfect dessert in a deep rounded plate. She cut slices with precision, spooning a golden sauce over them before passing them around. Toby's first bite melted in his mouth, the caramelized sugar the perfect foil for the rich custardy base.

When he'd finished, he waved off anything else. He couldn't remember the last time he'd eaten so much.

"I am wrapping some up for you take home."

"That's not necessary."

Her mom smiled. "Maybe not, but I would still like to."

Toby was kind of surprised that she hadn't

mentioned the baby beyond asking if they'd picked out names or not. Nor was there anything more said about his being the father. Then again, he wasn't out the door yet.

He glanced at his watch, surprised to find it was almost nine o'clock. "I need to head home pretty soon. I have an early morning."

Serena looked relieved. By the fact that he was leaving?

Gracia returned with a large bag. "This is for your lunch tomorrow." Then she kissed him on the cheek again.

"Thank you." To turn it down would seem ungrateful, and somehow he wondered if he'd be allowed to even leave the apartment without the bag of goodies.

Serena said in low tones, "I'll walk you to the door."

When they got there, he looked at her. "Well, that was a lot less painful than it could have been. She didn't ask any difficult questions."

There was a long pause before she finally responded. "Yeah, I noticed that. And to be honest, it kind of has me worried."

CHAPTER NINE

TOBY MET HER in Gary's office. He was right. The OB-GYN was discreet. When she'd told him that Toby would be joining her at the appointment, he'd arranged for them to come in another entrance at the building where his private practice was located and to wait in one of the exam rooms.

She was grateful. She knew there were Lamaze classes and so forth that she'd have to go through, and while Toby was coming to this appointment, she was reserving judgment about his being her birthing partner.

She didn't even know if he'd accept the role anyway.

She hadn't wanted to rock the boat, because things between them were actually not so bad right now. But she had a feeling it was because they were both on their best behavior. Kind of like Parker had been during the early days of their courtship.

Why had she thought of that? She and Toby weren't dating or even in a relationship.

But they were having a baby together.

She glanced at him to find he was staring at something on the wall. When she looked over there, she spied a large baby-development poster that showed the stages of pregnancy. There was a tension in him that made her uneasy. One that she hadn't sensed at dinner with her mom. Was he having second thoughts about all of this?

"You don't have to be here, you know."

He was the one who'd asked to come, but maybe this was all happening too fast for him. It wasn't like she could slow the process down, though. But his tension was spreading to her, and Serena wasn't sure she wanted to go through this with each and every appointment.

"I know."

Not quite the reassuring words she might have hoped for, like *I'm here because I want to be here*. Maybe she needed to talk to him afterward.

And tell him what? That he needed to

shape up and act happy or he couldn't come anymore?

The last thing she wanted from him was an act. She'd already experienced that before, and she could really do without it. She wanted her pregnancy to be a thing of wonder, where she anticipated each new stage—just like on that poster, where the mother-to-be was smiling—she'd rather it not be a stressful mess of wondering if Toby was regretting his decision to be a part of this. And she wondered about that each and every day. Today, he was giving her even more reason to wonder.

He could be funny and charming. But he could also be distant and hard to communicate with. Like right now.

He could be sexy as hell, and he could also shut down with a speed that made her head spin.

Wasn't she like that as well?

Maybe. But not about this. She was anxious to see what the appointment would bring. She wanted to know everything. The baby's size. How they were doing. If the baby was developing normally.

And she wanted to know the gender as soon as they could tell.

Did he?

She decided to tackle that question first, because Gary would eventually ask them. "Do you want to know if it's a boy or a girl when it comes time to find out?"

He glanced at her and then right back at the wall. The foot he had propped on his knee twitched a couple of times before quieting back down. "Whatever you think."

She blinked. What did he mean by that?

God, she was over thinking everything. But it felt like he was sucking every bit of joy out of the room. Out of her.

She decided not to ask him anything else. Maybe once Gary came in, he'd perk up.

Or maybe he wouldn't. But right now, she was regretting letting him come to the appointment at all.

A nurse came into the room, took her vitals and walked her down the hallway to weigh her. Toby opted to stay in the room, not even offering to accompany her. Which made sense, since they were trying to keep things quiet. But she halfway expected to find him gone when she reentered the space.

But he was still there. Still kind of broody, although he did send her a half-hearted smile, while his foot continued to bounce up and down on its perch. She could feel her heart rate speeding up to match its rhythm.

By the time Gary got there, she was a mass of conflicted feelings. Maybe she wasn't doing the right thing by having this baby. Maybe she should…

No. This was the right thing. For *her*. But maybe it wasn't for Toby. They hadn't really talked about the appointment over the last week and a half, and honestly he'd seemed fine about it. Until now.

Gary came in the room, took one look at Toby and said, "Everything okay?"

So she wasn't the only one who'd noticed it. She was glad, and yet, she wasn't. She'd kind of hoped she *was* being overly sensitive.

"Yep." He stood and shook the other man's hand. "Thanks for letting us come in the other entrance."

Serena felt herself shrink back in her chair. Was that it? Was he embarrassed that she was carrying his child? Despite the fact that she'd been as eager as he was to not let everyone know he was the father—at least not right away—this felt different somehow.

"Not a problem."

Gary turned to Serena as Toby took his seat again, crossing his leg and bouncing that damned foot again. She finally reached over and touched it. "Could you not do that, please? You're making me nervous."

"Got it." He uncrossed his legs and sat forward in his chair, elbows propped on his knees.

Well, hell. That wasn't any better.

She decided to ignore him.

"You ready to see what's happening with this little one?" Gary asked.

"Yes. More than ready." She forced a smile. Right now, she was just ready to get this over with and get out of this room. Away from Toby.

"Hop up on the table for me." She was already dressed in the hospital gown they'd given her when she'd first stepped foot in the room. And she'd never been so glad for the curtain that curved near the door and blocked Toby's view of her disrobing, which was ridiculous. But she was self-conscious all of a sudden, and she wasn't sure why.

She slid onto the table and somehow made it through the pelvic exam, feeling more and more regretful of Toby's presence in the room. He wasn't trying to be negative. He was just…quiet. Too quiet.

She missed the fun of the yoga class they'd taken together, missed the time they'd spent sitting on the beach—where the quiet had been a good thing, not this excruciating sensation that he'd rather be anywhere else in the world than here.

His words came back to her about not seeing himself having kids in the future. Well, the future was already here, and it was too late now. His world had been turned upside down in an instant.

"Okay, I'm going to do a sonogram, even though we won't be able to see a whole lot at this early stage. Certainly not enough to be able to see the baby's genitals, if you decide you want to know the sex.

Whatever you think.

That was just it. It wasn't whatever she thought. If he wanted to be involved in their child's life, she wanted his input. Not just about this, but about a lot of things. To have him sitting there, present and yet not present, was an awful sensation. One she didn't want their child experiencing.

Gary squirted warmed lubricating jelly on

her lower abdomen and then placed the scanner in the middle of the stuff. She immediately heard sounds of static from the wand being drawn across her belly. She was afraid to even look at Toby, afraid he'd still be staring at that poster on the wall and wishing he was anywhere but here.

"Okay, here we go."

Serena turned her attention to the screen, where she saw a black circle. In the middle of that dark space was a curved little creature. She immediately recognized the head. The tiny limbs that were starting to form. And she stopped dead when a distinct sound filled the room.

Blub-blub, blub-blub, blub-blub.

Just like the bounce of Toby's foot.

"We have a strong heartbeat." Gary glanced down at her with a smile.

Suddenly, she didn't care what Toby felt or didn't feel. An overwhelming sense of love filled her, growing to encompass this tiny start of life. But it didn't stop there—it soon spread outside of her belly and expanded its reach to include…

Toby.

Her eyes widened for a second. No, it was

just the wonder of seeing their baby for the first time. Of course she'd feel love for anyone in this room.

But she didn't love Gary Rollings. At least not in that way.

Something in her heart said the love she felt for Toby was different than what she felt for their baby. And that it was something that had been growing as irrevocably as the tiny scrap of life inside of her.

She kept her eyes on the screen, even as her heart wept over the impossibility of the situation. She wanted this baby.

But she also wanted him.

But he'd been clear. Very, very clear. While he was willing to entertain the idea of being a dad—something he might very well be rethinking right now—he'd made it clear that he didn't want anything more than that.

He'd even said he couldn't offer her a relationship. And she'd reassured him that that was okay. That she didn't expect one or want one either.

It hadn't been a lie. At the time. But it might very well be one now.

"Do you want me to print off an image? The 3D ultrasounds make it nice. You'll eventually be able to really see the baby's face."

"I would like one, thanks." She didn't ask Toby if he wanted one, and neither did Gary. It was pretty clear that he was either shell-shocked or...something else.

She was pretty shell-shocked herself. Not by the pregnancy. But by the discovery that she was in love with him.

And she had absolutely no idea what to do about it. One thing was for sure. She was not going to sit him down like she'd done with the pregnancy and tell him. She also wasn't sure she could sit here in an exam room month after month and try to hide her feelings from him. On the surgical floor, it was one thing. Things were busy and there wasn't a whole lot of time for introspection.

But here... Watching the growing development of her baby, she was afraid of seeing that mirrored in her feelings for him.

Maybe she needed to set up some boundaries and to cut off any time spent together outside of work and prenatal appointments.

That meant no more trips to Mission Beach. And that made her sad in a way she didn't understand.

"Do you know the due date, so I can try to arrange my schedule?"

Those were the first words out of Toby's mouth since they'd started the ultrasound. And the words had been a clinical dissection that cut to the heart of what was important to him: rearranging his schedule.

It should have made her happy that he seemed to confirm he still wanted to be a part of their baby's life. But she'd hoped for some kind of emotional response from him rather than something so detached.

"So conception... Do you know an exact day?"

Toby answered without hesitation. "May sixteenth."

Wow. She hadn't expected him to come up with the date that fast. And of course her brain was already putting all kinds of spin on that information. Was it that memorable? Was it a day he was hoping he could wish away?

She wouldn't know unless she asked. And she couldn't do that. Wouldn't do that. Not with the way she was feeling right now.

Gary checked something and then marked sections on the ultrasound. "That lines up with the size of the fetus. That puts you right around February sixth for a due date."

February sixth. Wow. It all of a sudden seemed right around the corner.

She finally chanced a glance at Toby and found him looking at his phone, tapping on the screen. Had he even looked at the ultrasound?

Surely…?

A sick sensation began crawling up her stomach. This wasn't right. She knew with a sinking heart that she couldn't go through this again.

It was obvious Toby was not happy being in this room. And right now, she'd rather he be anywhere but this room too.

She was not going to do this. Not this way.

It wasn't even like she'd asked him to come. He was the one who'd asked her if he could.

People change. Remember?

As if realizing something was wrong, Gary added, "Delivery times aren't set in stone, though. They're just a guideline."

They finished up the exam, which seemed to take forever. All she wanted to do was get out of this room. Get away from him. And do some heavy thinking. She would never take the baby away from Toby if he truly wanted to be a part of their life. But she would take anything involving her off the table.

Seeing as she was currently sitting on an exam table, that suddenly struck her as hilarious. And she giggled, the giggle changing to a laugh that lasted a few seconds too long. Toby and Gary were both looking at her like she'd lost her mind.

"Sorry. Something just struck me as funny."

Except it wasn't funny. Not right now, anyway. And she couldn't see the two of them laughing over this in the near future either.

So she'd just pull herself together and leave this room with all the dignity she could muster.

Toby had never had a panic attack before. But as he'd sat in that exam room with Serena yesterday, he'd come very close to having one. The walls had seemed to close in around him, the poster on the wall just making that sensation of time ticking by even stronger. February suddenly seemed right around the corner.

And he wasn't ready for this. Any of it.

He should probably go talk to Serena about it. He'd hoped she hadn't noticed anything was wrong, but there was no way she hadn't. He'd barely said two words. And when Gary had printed off one ultrasound image and handed it to Serena, he hadn't asked for one as well.

The images on that wall were burned into his head. The baby was chugging right along and would soon pass through all of those stages. And then things would no longer be hypothetical and abstract. They would be concrete, as in a living human being would settle into Gary's waiting hands.

And then Toby's entire life would change in ways he probably couldn't even imagine.

Ways that he'd tried to avoid.

Every visit to this office would drive that point home. Over and over and over.

Yet the alternative was unacceptable. That he would take the selfish way out and keep living just for himself.

Things weren't really all that cut and dried, but he tended to make them that way.

To top things off, Tanya had called him yesterday evening to tell him she was pregnant as well. Except she'd assured him it was Cliff's baby and not his. In case he heard about it through the grapevine. He had no idea which one that would be. Because while Paz Memorial had its own gossip chain, it didn't normally extend to neighboring hospitals, much less ones that were in other cities.

He'd told her he was happy for her. And he was. Her life seemed to have come together in a way that his hadn't. She was evidently in a loving relationship, which probably made things easier.

He was pretty sure if he'd offered marriage or some other form of commitment to Serena, she'd have cut him off.

She'd barely let him come to her appointment. And the thought of going to the next one… Well, it sent that crushing weight back to his stomach where it settled in for the foreseeable future.

He didn't think he could do it. Being a running companion was one thing. But being a parenting companion was another.

He was going to have to tell her. Or at least try to explain why he'd acted the way he had at her appointment. Gary asking if everything was okay pretty much told him that his panic had been just as noticeable as he'd thought it had been.

He just wasn't sure exactly how he was going to tell her. About any of it. The ball of fear that hung over him. The realization that he was right about fatherhood: he wasn't ready for it in the slightest.

But it was coming. Whether he was ready or not.

And somehow, he was going to have to figure out a way to come to terms with it.

Surgery on Monday morning was routine. A biker had laid his motorcycle down on the road and sustained an open fracture to his femur. And yet, as Serena handed Toby surgical instruments, it was anything but routine. She felt like she was standing over herself watching the surgery unfold without really being a part of it.

She realized then that was probably how Toby had felt at that appointment. That he'd been there, and yet, he hadn't been.

That made her sad and worried. She didn't want the man "going through the motions" when it came to his child's life. She wanted someone who was fully invested. Someone who felt they had skin in the game. Although the word *game* made her cringe. None of this was a game. It was very real. And far too important to take chances with.

So she was going to ask him to sit out for a couple of months from having anything to do with the pregnancy and then reevaluate how he felt afterward. If, at the end of that period, he felt relief, then she was going to do him a favor and ask him to step away from the situation, period—reassure him that she would be fine. She'd started off expecting to raise the baby on her own and had been reassured by both her mom and Avery that she wouldn't really be alone. There were people who wanted to help. Who really wanted to be there for her. And that's who she wanted gathered around her as she went through this process. Not someone who would come to resent everything to do with her and her baby.

She somehow got through the rest of the surgery and then slid away as soon as it was over to do a little thinking. She could do that while she saw to the patients and went about her day. She would have one final surgery at the end of the day, but it wasn't with Toby. It was with one of the orthopedists who had a specialized hand surgery coming up. Something that was new to Serena. Normally, she welcomed those kinds of cases—looked forward to them, since she learned so much from them.

But this time she wasn't. She kind of felt like she was in limbo, stuck between two worlds and trying to decide which one she wanted to choose. Which one she needed to choose.

Having this baby drag Toby along for the ride, or asking her mom to come and walk through the process with her.

She knew which one she wanted. But she didn't want it to involve an individual who said he'd be there but, in his heart of hearts, didn't really want to be there.

So after she was done with her final surgery, she was going to call him and ask to meet. And lay things out so there'd be no misunderstandings. On anyone's part.

Toby went to the beach. He'd needed the sounds of the ocean to lull him back to a place that wasn't so fraught with tension.

Except, when he got there, all he could

remember were the cries for help and that elderly man lying broken on the boardwalk.

He sat there for a few minutes before getting up and walking over to the spot where the man had lain. Roller-bladers and pedestrians streamed around him, most of them probably oblivious to what had happened there a little over a week ago. The man was long forgotten.

But not by him. And not by Serena either.

These days of her pregnancy would be forgotten too, eventually. And yet, right now, they were incredibly painful and drew up every insecurity he'd ever had. If it had been planned, maybe he'd feel differently. And yet, Serena seemed totally at ease with her decision.

So why wasn't he?

Checking his pocket for his phone, he realized he'd left it at home. That put an end to his plans for figuring this thing out. He needed to get home and make sure there were no emergencies that needed his attention.

So he got in his car and drove back to his apartment. The second he arrived, Porkchop greeted him at the door, winding around his ankles and begging for food. Not that he hadn't already fed her. She tended to beg no matter how many tidbits she received throughout the day.

"Wait a second, girl. I have to check something first."

He got his phone off the desk and scrolled through several messages before he realized his brain had skipped over one of them.

Backing up, he saw it there in red font. He'd missed a call from Serena. Two calls, actually, an hour apart.

Hell! Was there something wrong with her? With the baby?

Ignoring his cat for the moment, he pressed redial and waited as the phone on the other end rang once, twice, before a shaky voice responded with a single word.

"Hello?"

CHAPTER TEN

SHE MET HIM at the beach the following day, telling him she would drive separately. She couldn't see him wanting to take her home after she'd said what she had to say, although honestly, she thought some part of him would be relieved.

The thought of meeting at the hospital, even in the courtyard area, was unbearable. Even being the surgical nurse for his cases was hard right now. It brought back the fact that she cared about him in a way that had nothing to do with their being work colleagues. He'd been honest and told her the truth about how he felt, and she respected him for that. She wouldn't have wanted him to lie.

The weirdest thing was that she'd expected him to act one way, but then he'd acted in completely the opposite way—and it bothered her. Whereas Parker and her dad had a tendency to state what they wanted in no uncertain terms, Toby had expressed no interest whatsoever while they were at the doctor's office. In anything. Even when she'd joked that she wanted to be the one to choose the baby's name, he'd been fine with it.

He hadn't wanted a copy of the ultrasound. And while he'd programmed the delivery date into his phone, it was done as if it were simply another business appointment. The number of "not interested" signs was piling up fast. And she couldn't push through and pretend it didn't matter when he was right there beside her making it obvious that he'd prefer a token involvement rather than a real one.

But their child deserved more from him than that. And she would accept nothing less than true commitment.

This time, she brought a towel and sat on it as she waited for Toby to arrive. He wasn't late; she was early. But she'd wanted to make sure she was as composed as possible. She even had a cheat sheet tucked in her purse if she needed it that she could use to get all her points across. Although she couldn't see him arguing with anything she suggested.

Going back to work would be hard. The impulse to immediately quit and go somewhere else was still strong. Really strong. But she'd already been through that and decided she wasn't going to make any decisions until after the baby was born. To do anything else would be to act like her mom had with her dad—changing her plans because of something he wanted or didn't want instead of sticking to what she wanted.

She'd managed to work with Toby after sleeping with him. This would be no different, right?

Toby found her five minutes later studying her notes, which she quickly shoved into her pocketbook.

He dropped onto the sand beside her and looked at her. "Why couldn't you tell me whatever this is about over the phone?"

"Because I think it's better done in person." She realized she was using the same argument Toby had used about not telling her about Patient Doe's death over the phone. He'd been right, she thought now. About that, at least.

"Okay." He drew the word out in a way that said he didn't agree.

But it didn't matter if he agreed. She'd already made the decision. And she was going to make this about her rather than about what he had and hadn't done.

"I think I'd like to go to the rest of my doctor's appointments by myself."

He closed his eyes for a second before looking at her again. And yes, she could swear that was relief in expression. "Any particular reason?"

"Lots of them. But they all lead to the same place. That it's uncomfortable for me to have you there." She left out the part about its being due to his stilted behavior.

"I'm sorry if I've—"

"I think I would have felt the same way no matter what."

He waited a long time. "And the baby. Are you still going to let me into their life?"

"We—meaning both you and I together—can decide that after the baby gets here. In the meantime, I want you to think long and hard about what you want, because there won't be any fence-sitters. I don't have an option about being a parent—well, I do, but it's not one I want to explore. You can choose though. I know you said you wanted to be involved, but by not coming to my appointments, it'll give you a chance to reexamine your motivations for wanting to be involved. Whatever they are, don't let it be out of guilt. Because that isn't fair to the baby."

He didn't interrupt her. Didn't correct her. He just let her keep on talking until she was all done.

Then he nodded. "So let me see if I've got this straight. You don't want me at your appointments. And you want me to use the time to figure out if I really want to be involved in the baby's life or not."

"Yes."

"You're still coming to work. Is that correct?"

She looked at him. "Is that a problem for you?"

"No. But you're making it sound like you don't want us to be around each other until after the baby is born, and maybe not even then."

"We don't see each other all the time at work. So I don't have any plans to go anywhere."

His brows came together. "I don't remember asking you to."

"Okay. Just making sure." She paused. "Do you have anything to say?"

If she'd been hoping for him to argue with her, to say that's not what he wanted at all, she was sorely disappointed. Because his only comment was, "You'll let me know how things are going?"

"I think it'll be best if we don't talk about the baby at work at all."

"So I'm just to assume that no news means that everything is going as expected?"

She hesitated. "If I…lose the baby…" She almost couldn't get those words out. "I'll let you know."

She wasn't sure, but she thought he might have gone pale at her words. But that didn't make any sense. She'd made peace with their not being together—at least she hoped to hell she had—but she had to accept that, just like folks who were divorced with kids, they would always be in each other's lives in some way, shape or form because of this baby.

Unless he decided he didn't want to be involved in any way. A part of her hoped that would be the case. Because then she could stay or leave the hospital and even the city without giving any thought to him or his access to his child.

He'd been looking out to sea, but when she said that, he turned to look at her, his eyes intent on hers. "I want to let you know that whatever happens, I don't want you to lose this baby. I want this little one to be healthy and have a happy life. I'm just not…"

He didn't finish his sentence, but it didn't matter. None of the myriad combination of words would make whatever his thought was into something positive. But at least she was finally getting some honesty out of him. And, whatever it was, *not* was at the center of it.

Not…good father material.

Not…prepared to father a child.

Not…willing to be involved.

They all basically meant the same thing.

"It's okay, Toby. Which is why it's better this way. You let me know when you've made a decision one way or the other."

"I told you that you wouldn't have to go through this alone."

The words were like a spear that hit her

midchest. She'd thought about that, but that first appointment had made her take a closer look at his offer. "Sometimes you're alone, even when there are other people around."

He averted his gaze, looking out over the water. "I'm sorry if you felt that way."

She shrugged. "It's just easier to go it alone than…" Than worry about whether the other person is dreading being there. But she left that part unsaid. He'd gotten her point. It was better to leave it at that.

With that, she stood and shook her towel out. "Well, that's all I wanted to say. I'll see you at work."

"Yes."

He didn't get up or offer to walk with her back to her car, just sat there looking straight ahead.

It was easier this way. There was no need to confess her feelings or pressure him to keep coming to her appointments. The first one was too awful. Too painful. It reminded her of all she wanted but couldn't have.

She walked away, heading toward her car. Her vision was blurred, and her head suddenly was stuffed full of second thoughts and wishes that there'd been another way.

There hadn't been. And he'd seemed to confirm that by his response.

He was relieved. Even if she was anything but.

She was true to her word. Serena saw him at work but made no effort to engage in small talk. She treated him like any other doctor she'd worked with. Maybe even a little more formally. Because he noticed she did engage in chit chat with other doctors. With Toby, though, she normally just nodded and did her job, keeping her head down whenever possible.

And she rarely looked him in the eye. He found he missed that the most.

Hell, he shouldn't have cared. She'd made it pretty clear that she didn't want him involved in her life. At all. She'd said it was up to him, but she sure hadn't made it sound that way. So he was bracing for her to shut him out of her life completely. Including out of his child's life.

He'd thought that was what he'd wanted as well when he'd sat there in that exam room. But a hard ball of bile had sat at the back of his throat for a week now. A week since they'd talked on the beach. A week and two days since her initial doctor's appointment.

Mabel Tucker was due to come in today for her third and final follow-up. He didn't call Serena and let her know, because, well, she didn't want to be around him. She'd made that very clear. So he doubted she would want to be there for anything involving him. Even for a patient she liked.

He sat in his office, looking at the chair they'd made love in. He'd had it professionally cleaned, saying he wanted to start doing that periodically. But it didn't matter how many steamers came in. He would always picture her kneeling over him, her butterfly tattoo clearly visible.

Maybe he'd have to throw those ones out and get some new chairs. Chairs that didn't remind him of her.

Sometimes you're alone, even when there are other people around.

He hadn't understood what she'd meant. Until now. Until he'd stood in a surgical suite with her nearby and felt totally disconnected from her. Totally alone. Just like he had felt during his childhood. And he'd realized how very much he'd missed out on growing up.

The old man from the boardwalk came to mind. He'd had a crowd gathered around him. And yet, he'd been totally and utterly alone. Unknown by any one of those people. Unknown by him. By Serena.

Was that really who he wanted to be? Someone people recognized but didn't really know?

There was a knock at the door and his heart sped up for a second only to thud to nothing when he opened the door and found Mabel and Tom standing there.

There must have been something in his face, because Tom spoke up. "Did we have the right time?"

"Yes, of course. Sorry."

Had he really expected Serena to be there, telling him she was sorry and that she really wanted him to come to her appointments after all?

A little flicker of shock lit up inside of him. He kind of had. Why else would his heart have reacted the way it had?

He was an idiot. He was the one who should be going to her and asking for her forgiveness rather than the other way around. It was because of him that she'd felt alone and unsupported. Maybe after this appointment, he'd go find her and see if he couldn't somehow make this right.

He ushered the couple into his office, and they sat in the chairs across from his desk, making him swallow.

"I have a new piece of bling." Mabel shook her wrist and a silver bracelet jingled there. Holding it out, she let him look at it.

"This is a fancy one."

It was a medical alert bracelet, but the links and attachment were swirled and decorative, the nameplate looking more like an oval piece of silver than the utilitarian versions he'd seen in the past.

"I love bracelets, so I researched them."

He read the inscription on the plate, and it had all the pertinent information in clear lettering, so he couldn't complain about it. Not that he would, unless he felt it wouldn't be clearly seen by emergency services.

"It's very nice. And I'm glad to see you wearing it." It had been more than four weeks since her surgery. "How are you feeling?"

"A lot better than last week. I feel like I've finally made it over the hump."

"You might still feel better, but it's easy to

overdo it, so take it easy for a couple more weeks.

"I'm trying. But it's not easy."

"Did you get the immunizations we talked about?"

She nodded. "Yep. Last week. But…"

"But?"

"Are we cleared to, um, resume relations?"

"Yes, as long as you're not having pain." He paused. "I know you guys talked about wanting to start a family, but I'd like you to hold off for a month or two until we see how your body adjusts to life without a spleen."

"We weren't planning to start trying right away. The thought of having someone push on my stomach during an exam is still a little daunting."

"I know. Fortunately, we won't have to do that today, unless you're noticing anything abnormal."

"No. Nothing. The scar is starting to turn white, though. It's been bloodred ever since it was done."

"That's good news, actually."

Tom took her hand and squeezed. "I'm just glad she's here, alive and well."

"So am I." Mabel's eyes were no longer

black, and looking at her, you would have never guessed that she'd been on the brink of death from a car accident just over a month ago. She was very lucky.

And lucky she didn't have to go through her recovery alone, without emotional support.

His gut spasmed.

Yes, she was very lucky. Because unlike that man on the boardwalk, she had someone who made sure of that. Someone who hadn't left her side and had been there in ways that went beyond the physical. Something Toby hadn't done for Serena. Or her baby.

Why?

He blinked, suddenly realizing why. Because he'd fallen in love with her. And being around her made him want things he'd said he'd never want again: companionship...a family.

Was that why he'd been so struck by the stuff he'd seen in the waiting room? By the picture of developing babies that reminded him that even if he was there for the baby, Serena probably didn't want him around her?

Hell, she'd made that pretty clear on the beach.

But maybe that had had more to do with his attitude than hers. She'd been happy enough to have him there, until she'd actually experienced his being there. He'd been an idiot at Gary's office, to be honest. He'd been uncommunicative to the point of being rude. He hadn't been present. Not in an emotional way. Instead, he'd held himself apart.

To protect himself from being hurt?

Maybe. That and out of fear, for sure. The thought of becoming a father like his own still terrified him.

Was it because he was afraid Serena would take off on him, like Tanya had done? Or was it more about his fear of becoming the kind of parent that made you feel alone, even when they were there? Like Serena had mentioned on the beach.

Well, his fear had made that a self-fulfilling prophesy. He was afraid. So he'd held himself back. Until he hadn't been there at all. He wouldn't blame Serena for wanting him out of there.

And if he'd participated in that appointment?

He was pretty sure that things would be different now. Serena was not Tanya. She was the type to stay in there and gut it out. As long as she knew the other person would do the same.

Would he?

Tom was looking at him, and he realized he'd missed something they'd said.

"Sorry, I was thinking of another case. What did you say?"

"I asked if there was anything else we should be looking for from here on out."

"Gotcha. Like I said before, just be careful of exposing yourself to communicable illnesses. And wait at least a month or so before trying to start a family."

"That sounds easy enough."

Didn't it, though? Lots of challenges could be solved by a simple set of steps. People just weren't always willing to do the work.

Like him?

Yep. Just like him.

And what was the work?

To tell Serena that he cared about her. That he cared about the baby. And then wait and see how she reacted.

Could he do it?

The question wasn't *could*. It was *would*. *Would* he do it?

He and the Tuckers said their goodbyes, and the couple headed out the door, hand in hand. Maybe Toby needed to be brave enough to face life head on, like Mabel and Tom. To do that, he needed to go find Serena and...

Do what?

He wasn't sure. But he hoped he would know as soon as he set eyes on her.

Closing the door to his office, he headed down the hallway toward the nurses' station only to spy a figure rushing toward him. Serena. Her face was streaked with tears, making a chill go through him. He quickened his step, and when he reached her, he took hold of her arms.

"What is it?"

She sobbed, putting a hand to her mouth. "Toby, I—I think I might be losing the baby."

CHAPTER ELEVEN

THE TRIP TO Gary's office was made in complete silence as Toby gripped the wheel and dodged traffic for the two blocks that it took to reach the private practice. His heart was stuffed with regret over all the things he hadn't said. The things that might be too late to say now.

This time, Toby didn't worry about going in any back entrance, just gripped her hand and rushed her into the building.

As soon as the receptionist saw his face, she picked up her phone and called someone. A few seconds later, a nurse motioned them to come through the door, bypassing everyone else in the waiting room.

Gary appeared, his face showing concern. "I know this isn't a social visit, so tell me what's going on."

"I'm bleeding. And I'm afraid—"

"How much blood?"

"Not a ton, but—"

"Let's get you into a gown and on the table. If I even suspect something is happening, you're going right back to the hospital."

He looked at Toby, who nodded, feeling numb with fear.

"Understood," he said.

Gary left the room and Toby helped her undress and get into the fabric gown, seeing for himself that there was blood in her panties. He swallowed a lump, wanting to say so much yet knowing now was not the time.

The exam was quick and involved a physical exam, where Gary pronounced that the cervix looked intact, although there was a hint of bloody discharge. "It's not necessarily indicative of a miscarriage. Sometimes there is a little spotting, but I want to do another sonogram and make sure everything looks okay inside."

A nurse came in and got things ready, and then the wand moved over Serena's bare abdomen.

This time, when Toby heard the baby's heartbeat, a sense of overwhelming relief washed over him like a tsunami, completely different from the fear he'd felt last time in this room.

"How is everything?" The words came out before he could stop them.

"Everything looks good. The baby's heart rate is right on track."

"Thank God." He couldn't stop himself from dropping into a chair and putting his head between his hands. He took a moment or two to calm his erratic breathing, the adrenaline that had gotten him here deserting him completely. His legs felt like blocks of cement, and he wasn't sure how he was going to get them to carry him out of this room.

Serena's voice came to him. "So I'm not miscarrying?"

That made his head come back up as he waited for Gary to make his pronouncement.

"There's no sign of that. Sometimes, especially with first pregnancies, we see a little bit of spotting and never discover any real reason for it. We'll culture a swab and make sure there's no sign of infection, but there's no more active bleeding, so we're going to assume all is well. I want you to go home and put your feet up and let me know if it comes back."

"Thank you. I don't know what I'd do if..." The shaking of her voice got Toby staggering up out of his chair, and he gripped her hand hard.

Serena looked up in his face with a look of confusion. He couldn't blame her. He'd been a complete jerk the last time they were in this room. But he wanted to change that as soon as they got out of here.

Gary shook both of their hands and told them to call him if there was any more bleeding. Toby promised they would.

They.

As in both of them.

Because he hoped to hell she would be willing to give him a chance to explain. To say that he'd come to a decision. That he wanted to be involved in not only the baby's life, but also in hers.

"I'll take you home."

She nodded, getting dressed quickly. "I feel so stupid."

"Don't. Gary didn't treat this lightly, so that should tell you something. I was just so glad to hear that heartbeat."

"You were?" She stopped and looked at him again.

"I was, and I—"

His phone rang and when he glanced down at the readout, he saw that it was the hospital.

"It's okay. Answer it. We can talk later."

He pressed a button. "Renfro here."

He listened as one of the ER doctors asked where he was and if he could make it back to the hospital as soon as possible. They had an emergency, and he was the only on-call trauma specialist scheduled for this afternoon.

He glanced at Serena, who must have seen something in his face.

"Go. I told Avery what was happening, and he was supposed to meet me here. I didn't even think to call him back and tell him that you'd decided to come with me. He can take me home."

Said as if she hadn't expected him to even offer. Hell, he had so much to apologize for. But it had to wait.

"Are you sure?" He told the hospital he would be there in five minutes, then hung up.

"Yes. Absolutely."

He gripped her hand and gave it a squeeze.

"I'd like to talk to you, but since it's already four o'clock, I have a feeling it won't be until tomorrow now. I want you to rest this evening and get a good night's sleep. Can you promise to call me if you need me?"

"I will."

He carried her hand to his mouth and kissed her palm. "Then how about we meet up at your yoga spot in the morning?"

She nodded. "I'd like that. Now go, so you can take care of that emergency."

With his heart feeling just a little bit lighter that it had all week, he headed out the door.

Daisies lined the perimeter of the little area of Balboa Park.

Had last night been a dream? Toby had seemed so different. Had said he wanted to talk to her. And when he'd kissed her palm, she'd almost hoped...

Well, she hadn't been able to stop thinking about that all night. And she was horrified by how hard she'd been wishing that there was more to that kiss than met the eye.

But now, there was no sign of him. Although this spot didn't look the same. Nor was there any sign of a yoga class being set up. Serena stopped, her beach bag with her yoga mat and change of clothes over her shoulder. She must have stopped at the wrong place.

She backed out of the area and glanced around at the nearby benches. Yes, this was the right spot. She and Toby had jogged out of here as soon as they'd finished doing the class that day.

Had they discontinued the classes? Surely Veronica would have sent her a text saying so if that were the case.

Besides, Toby had asked her to meet her here. Had he changed his mind?

She went back into the little cut back area and looked again. Still no sign of anyone. And although Serena tended to run early, she'd never gotten here before the instructor.

And although there were always palm trees, the pots of daisies were new, unless they were planning on planting some in the area.

She stood there for a minute longer before realizing someone was behind her. Whirling around, she saw Toby standing there, another basket of daisies in the crook of his arm.

"W-where's my yoga class?"

"It's still meeting. Just a few yards away. What I have to say, I want to say to you alone."

She took a small step backward in confusion.

His finger circled her wrist. "Stay. Please." His touch was warm and soft, the slide of his thumb on her inner wrist making her pulse jump all over again.

She glanced at the potted plant in his hands. "Are you responsible for the flowers?"

"You said they were your favorite."

So he'd had all of these brought in? Had asked the yoga class to meet somewhere else? She swallowed. He surely hadn't done this for the benefit of the instructor or the other students. He'd done it for...her?

Why? Unless...

That kiss on her palm.

No. That couldn't be right.

"What's this about, Toby?" Her voice shook, but there was nothing she could do about that right now. God. She didn't want him to say anything if it wasn't what she was beginning to hope for.

"This is about me. Apologizing. And hoping you'll forgive me."

"Because of yesterday?"

"Yes, but not because you thought you were losing the baby. I met with Mabel and Tom yesterday afternoon and had already decided to go look for you and apologize." His eyes closed for a second. "And then you came running down the hall, and I thought my whole world was ending."

"You did?"

He nodded and then pulled in a deep breath. "The first time I sat in that doctor's office, I kept thinking about all the reasons I couldn't have a family. Why I'd make such a horrible dad. And it became this huge macabre ghost that I couldn't see past."

"But why did you feel like that?"

"My parents are nothing like your mom, Serena. They're—it's hard to explain. They're not demonstrative people. And I sometimes find myself being like that too. Having a hard time calling up my feelings and letting them out."

"I noticed that in Gary's office the first time. I sensed you didn't want to be there. But yesterday…"

"Yesterday, that all changed. And not just

because I thought you were losing the baby. I realized I didn't want to lose *you*."

"And so…?"

"I realized at Mabel Tucker's appointment yesterday that I want what she and her husband have. The companionship that means they don't have to experience being alone even when other people are around."

"But you can only have what they have if you—"

"Love each other? Yes. And I understood right then… I love you, Serena. I love this baby—even though I'm scared out of my wits that I won't be good at being a father."

"Are you saying all of this because you think it's what I want to hear?"

He shook his head. "I'm saying it because it's true." The fingers still encircling her wrist moved down, sliding over her palm in a way that half tickled, half aroused her, reminding her of the firm lips he'd pressed to it yesterday.

Could this really be happening? She hadn't wanted to see him anymore, because she'd also realized she loved him and that it was an impossible situation.

And yet, he'd been the first person she'd

run to when she thought she was losing the baby. Because she loved him too.

She looked around the space. Hundreds of baskets of her favorite flower. "How did you even get these all here?"

"I rented a van yesterday afternoon and went to a flower market."

"Seriously?" She tried to picture him walking around and searching the place for daisies. Her heart swelled to bursting. Because she really could see him doing that. At least, the Toby from yesterday at the doctor's office. "What are you planning to do with them all afterward?"

"I'm donating them to the park to be planted around this area. I want them to be a permanent reminder of how I feel about you every time we come here to do yoga."

"We?"

He nodded. "If you want me there." He took a step closer and cupped her chin. "Because I want to be there. I want to be there for all of it. Your prenatal appointments. Your cravings—if you even get those."

"Oh, I do. Believe me."

"I want to be there for this baby's birth and for every event thereafter. But most of all, I want to be there for you. I realized that I didn't want to be John Doe, standing alone in the midst of a crowd."

She nodded. "I thought the same thing about John Doe. It was one of the reasons I didn't want you at my appointments. I decided I wanted to forge meaningful relationships, like the one I have with Avery and my mom and brother. And when I thought you weren't able or willing to give me that… I couldn't bear to see you there month after month just going through the motions."

"And now? Do you think you can forge a meaningful relationship with me?"

Her fingers came up to touch his face. "I do. But only if you truly mean it."

"I've never meant anything more in my life."

He took her yoga mat out of her bag and laid it on the ground. Then he coaxed her to sit down next to him.

Daisies surrounded them. Beautiful. Meaningful. And Toby had done it all for her.

He kissed her. "I love you, Serena."

"I love you too, Toby. So very much."

His fingers sifted through her hair. "Can I come to the appointments again?"

"Yes. As long as you're serious about them not bothering you."

"I can't promise they won't affect me. But I imagine that's going to be in good ways from here on out."

"Does this mean I have to go jogging with you too?"

"Only if you want to."

She grinned. "I think I'm going to like it a whole lot better now."

"If they can't find John Doe's family, I'd like to unofficially adopt him as ours. To see that he gets a decent burial with a marker."

"I'd love that." She hesitated for a minute. "And I'd like to name our baby Faith. Because it's going to take a lot of faith to get us where we're going."

"Faith. I like that. But what if it's a boy?"

"We'll cross that bridge when we come to it. But we'll do it together."

He set his daisies down next to the mat and gently leaned in to kiss her. Her insides quivered as his lips skimmed over hers again and again. Thank God this was a private—

"Excuse me. Do you know where they moved the yoga class to?"

The voice caused them to shoot apart.

Serena laughed when she saw the woman's befuddled glance as she looked around the space.

"I'll take you to it," Toby offered.

After going with Toby to lead the woman to the day's temporary yoga space, Serena smiled at the other people who were already working on their poses. Several of them stopped to clap when they saw her. One said, "Will you be joining us?"

"Not today, ladies. I've got some other things to do." She glanced behind her to find that Toby had followed her over. "And they include this guy here. But I'll be back."

His brows went up, probably at her public acknowledgment of their relationship. But right now, she wanted the whole world to know. She loved him. And he'd said he loved her.

They left the yoga class to its own devices and wandered past the other spot hand in hand. "Oh, wait," she said. She zipped in and picked up her yoga mat and the one pot of daisies that Toby had been carrying.

"What's that for?"

"It's a memory of today. So that in the

morning, I don't wake up and wonder if it really happened."

"You'll remember, Serena. Because I plan to wake up next to you tomorrow. And every other day. For the rest of our lives. If you'll let me."

"Oh, yes, I'll let you," she breathed. "I'll let you do that, and so much more."

This time when they kissed, it was a pledge that they would indeed be there for each other. And the promise that neither of them would ever have to be alone again.

EPILOGUE

SERENA'S MOM FIDDLED with her veil and then gave her a peck on the cheek. She then bent over to kiss the fluff of hair on the head that peeked out of the baby wrap carrier Serena had strapped to her chest.

She and Toby had decided they didn't need a traditional wedding—not all of it, anyway. So they'd opted to wait for Faith to be born and to make her a part of the ceremony. Instead of a maid of honor, Serena had asked Avery to be a *person* of honor instead. And her mother would walk her down the aisle.

It was perfect. Every little bit of it.

She and Toby had both had to make personal sacrifices to make their relationship work. He was fully committed to her and the baby—something he proved daily through his actions. And he claimed it was not a sacrifice at all. She and Toby had both gone through counseling and had learned to listen and communicate, to make sure they each had the other's best interests at heart. They were still learning. But it was working for them.

"Are you ready?" her mom asked.

"More than ready. We'd better do this while she's still sleeping."

Gracia adjusted the train of Serena's wedding gown and snugged the baby a little more firmly in the white knit carrier that had been trimmed with some of the lace from her veil.

Then she opened the doors to the hospital chapel, and they stepped into the tiny anteroom.

Toby was at the front, looking dazzling in his black tux. He was accompanied by Paz Memorial's chaplain and Avery, and they were chatting with each other and hadn't yet seen her. A handful of friends and family, including his parents and Serena's brother, were scattered in the chapel's seating area, while daisies filled the space. It reminded her of when she'd arrived at yoga class to find he'd tucked pots of the flowers among the greenery, making it a place of wonder. And love.

Toby noticed her first.

Holding the baby against her with one arm and gripping her mom's hand with the other, they slowly made their way down the center of the chapel as the music played. Toby's incredible eyes locked on hers, and he mouthed *I love you* as they drew near. She smiled at him, happiness filling her to overflowing.

It was beautiful and small and serene, just like she'd wanted.

Arriving at the front, he came down the step to stand beside her, waiting there while Gracia kissed them both. Serena handed her daisy bouquet, made by her mom, to Avery, who nodded his approval.

"Do you have the rings?"

Avery reached in his pocket and withdrew two rings. One a solid black band and one in silver set with emeralds. While the chaplain read the words of their vows and waited as they each repeated them back to him, Serena could barely believe this was happening. But it was. She was the luckiest girl on the planet. She'd expected to have a baby and raise it on her own. She would have been grateful for just that. But she'd gotten so much more. She'd gained a partner who would make sure she didn't run this particular race on her own. He'd be right there with every footfall, through happiness and exhaustion, through frustration and joy. And Serena wouldn't have it any other way.

"By the power vested in me by the State of California, I pronounce you husband and wife. You may kiss each other."

Toby wrapped his arms around her and the baby and held them for a long, long time, whispering how happy she'd made him. How he hadn't known what he truly wanted in life until he'd almost lost it. Then, and only then, did he kiss her softly on the mouth, taking his time and making heat simmer in her belly.

Avery handed Serena's flowers back to Toby, since she didn't have enough hands to juggle everything, and they turned and faced their family and friends, who cheered and called for them to kiss again. Serena was happy to oblige, letting go of his hand so she could pull his head down. She put everything in that kiss—all of her love, hope and dreams.

They would quietly go back to Toby's apartment and feed Porkchop and start living the life they'd dreamed of. No honeymoon. They'd already kind of, sort of, had one of those in Mexico almost ten months ago. Right now, all they needed was each other.

Walking down the aisle, they were showered by rose petals from those in attendance. And Faith chose that moment to give a chirping cry, stirring in the carrier. Her blue eyes, so like her daddy's, blinked open, and she fixed her mommy with a look that said they didn't have much time. And feeding her in this gown might prove challenging.

It was okay. Life itself was challenging. But it was also good. So very good.

Serena planned to spend every day focusing on that. And Toby would be right there with her. Each and every day—as far into the future as she could see.

His arm tightened around her, and he

swept her out of the chapel, out of the hospital and into the wide, wide world. Where anything was possible. And where love was everything.

* * * * *

*Look out for the next story in the
California Nurses duet*

Nurse with a Billion Dollar Secret
by Scarlet Wilson

*If you enjoyed this story, check out these
other great reads from Tina Beckett*

**The Vet, the Pup and the Paramedic
A Family Made in Paradise
From Wedding Guest to Bride?**

All available now!